The Secret of the Silver Lockets

John Lester, fifteen-year-old son of a well-known actor, is on holiday on the Scottish coast with his fourteen-year-old cousin, Michelle Ward. When, on their way to a picnic, they help a weary motorcyclist who gives Michelle a small present in return, they never imagine that it will lead to their becoming involved in an adventure which takes them up and down Britain and even abroad, as they try to link together the pieces of a puzzling mystery involving silver lockets which seem to interest more than one gang of crooks. The cousins' quiet holiday is drastically transformed as they find themselves caught in a web of dangerous and often horrifying situations, face the evil schemes of a murderous gang and encounter the terrible Tigress. As new faces constantly appear in the mystery, the cousins desperately try to work out what is going on, while facing perils greater than they have ever experienced in their lives.

Best Wishes
to Sheila

Lindsay Brown

Also by Lindsay Brown in Piccolo
The Treasure of Dubarry Castle

Lindsay Brown

The Secret
of the Silver Lockets

Piccolo Books

First published 1980 by Robert Hale Ltd
This Piccolo edition published 1982 by Pan Books Ltd,
Cavaye Place, London SW10 9PG
© Lindsay Brown 1980
ISBN 0 330 26628 4
Phototypeset by Input Typesetting Ltd, London SW19 8DR
Printed and bound in Great Britain by
Collins, Glasgow

*To my dear Grandparents
and Godparents*

Author's Note

I should like to express my thanks to my friend Rhona MacDonald, who supplied me with much extremely useful information about Norway, without which I should not have been able to attempt to set part of the story there.

I am also very grateful to both my parents, who provided invaluable help with the revision of the book after it had been accepted for publication, and to my brother Rupert, for gallantly putting up with endless discussions of scenes and characters, while revision was in progress, in his usual cheerful way.

Contents

chapter one

The Mysterious Traveller

'It's *freezing*!' yelled John, splashing back to the shore as fast as he could. Michelle stood on a rock on the shingle beach laughing as her cousin waded out of the cold sea, shivering. She flung him a towel. John wrapped it round his tanned shoulders and picked his way over the shingle to Michelle. He sat down beside her on a rock which was coated with cool sunlight.

'Well, whose idea was it to have a nice early morning swim?' mused Michelle, her long chestnut hair rippling in the warm breeze.

'Hmm. I don't see why *I* had to play the part of a guinea-pig and test the water, though,' muttered the blond, good-looking John, rubbing himself dry vigorously. 'Pass me my shirt and sandals, will you? Thanks.'

Michelle looked out over the grey-blue water which glistened in the light of the newly risen sun.

'The sea certainly *looks* inviting,' she remarked.

'Yes,' John agreed, 'but I'm surprised the fish aren't all lying in refrigerated blocks of ice on the seabed. Come on. I'm hungry. Let's go back to the house for breakfast.'

They made their way up a narrow sandy path which wound up to the clifftop.

'I wonder if Mum and Dad have boarded the boat to France yet,' said Michelle. Her parents were going on a holiday abroad while John's parents had arranged to take a long cruise. This had given cousins John, who was fifteen, and fourteen-year-old Michelle a chance to meet for the first time in three years and to spend a holiday together on the south-west Scottish coast near Ballantrae.

It did not take them long to reach the holiday cottage where they were staying with the friendly Mrs Hodge, the housekeeper. John's real home was in Leicester but his father, who was the successful actor, Gareth Lester, also owned this spacious and pleasant cottage on the coast. Michelle's home was in a pleasant area in the suburbs of Glasgow. Her father, Andrew Ward, was a police inspector and her mother taught in a primary school. The cousins had always enjoyed each other's company and liked to meet as often as possible in school holidays.

Mrs Hodge had set up tables and chairs in the front garden. ' 'Twas too nice a day to eat indoors,' she explained as the cousins crossed the lawn. 'Had a good swim, eh?' The teenagers exchanged smiles.

'Well, it was a bit chilly,' replied John. 'I'll just go and change into some shorts.' He scurried indoors and Michelle sat down, helping herself to a morning roll. Mrs Hodge was a podgy, pleasant woman of around forty, hardly ever seen not wearing her apron. Her brow creased into a mock frown as John approached the table carrying his transistor radio.

'Now now,' she begged.

'It's much pleasanter without that thing blaring away,' protested Michelle, ' – at least, while we're having breakfast.'

'Come now. I'll have it on ever so quietly,' promised John in persuasive tones, taking a seat. 'There's a fabulous song on.' He took Mrs Hodge's smile as consent and spent nearly all of breakfast-time with his ear to the transistor.

It was Michelle's idea to have a picnic that warm day. They gathered together the necessary articles while Mrs Hodge packed the food. The house-keeper knew of a small sandy beach not far off and they set off under a burnished blue sky. The road was deserted and they walked at its side over stones and tangled grass. John trailed behind slightly with his transistor to his ear and his free hand swinging to the beat of the music, despite a picnic basket hung over the crook of the same arm.

'Michelle,' said Mrs Hodge in a voice which was loud enough for John to hear, 'what does John find in that raucous racket?' Michelle glanced back with a mischievous grin at John, who was pretending not to listen.

'Well, you see, Mrs Hodge, being such a terrible singer, it consoles him to hear someone who is almost as bad at singing as he is.' John glared at her, but with a twinkle in his eye.

The cousins often teased each other, but neither

minded. John was full of fun and always trying to be witty. Being blond and handsome he was a little vain but not as much as might be expected. Although he could be sullen at times, on the whole he was cheerful and made the most of life.

At that moment he was so involved with his current favourite song that he did not notice Michelle start as she caught sight of a disturbing spectacle. A man in a dusty and dirt-streaked brown anorak was struggling along the road, leaning heavily on the saddle of a somewhat battered motorbike. He dragged one leg behind him and the sweat trickling over his face was mingled with blood and grime. Dry blood stained his trouser-leg and his shoulders were hunched. Mrs Hodge followed Michelle's anxious glance and both of them quickened their pace, alarmed. The man stopped by a couple of dry, thin trees, unable to go any farther. Panting incessantly, he was half sprawled over his motorbike as Michelle and Mrs Hodge reached him. He raised his weary head and gazed at them with bloodshot grey eyes. John suddenly noticed what was going on. He flicked off his transistor and joined Michelle.

'Can we help you?' Mrs Hodge asked in anxious tones.

'Your motorbike looks in pretty bad shape,' commented John. 'Did you have an accident?'

The man nodded. 'My name is Evans,' he told them in a deep, hoarse voice. 'I was –'

'Wait a minute,' exclaimed Mrs Hodge. 'You can't give us your life story in this state. Sit down

12

over here. Michelle, get the drinks out of the smallest basket.'

She put a steadying arm around Evans's shoulders and helped him to the roadside, where he slithered to the ground with his back against a tree. John wheeled the motorbike to the other tree and leaned it against the trunk. There was a rucksack strapped to the back of the vehicle. They squatted round the weary man and Michelle poured out some juice which she handed him. He gulped it down gratefully and wiped the sweat from his forehead with the back of a grimy hand.

'You are very kind.' He nodded with appreciation at Mrs Hodge's plump, merry face as she pushed back the greasy dark hair from over his eyes and unzipped his brown anorak, to reveal a shirt discoloured with perspiration. 'I'd better tell you what happened,' Evans began. 'You see, I'm a botanist and I'm writing' – he coughed – 'a book on Scottish plants and flowers. I'm particularly interested in the plants in the Highlands and I was travelling there on my motorbike. I had an accident and fell off the bike about half an hour ago. I hurt my leg. The bike only suffered a few scratches but I was scared to start riding in case I fell off again because of my leg. I was miles from any village. You are the first people I've seen since the accident. I was hoping to find help, but now I'm so exhausted I just can't go on any more . . .'

The pathetic voice would have melted a heart of stone. Mrs Hodge and John gently rolled up the man's mud-splattered trouser-leg and examined the

13

wound. Michelle winced at the unpleasant sight. It was not a deep scrape but it was expansive and grit and gravel were mixed with the blood.

Mrs Hodge pulled a face and asked, 'Have you hurt yourself anywhere else?'

'Not much,' Evans replied. 'Just a few bruises and scratches.'

'Can you walk?'

He shrugged uneasily. 'I – I don't think so. I – er . . .'

'Don't worry,' Mrs Hodge said soothingly. 'John will run home and fetch the first-aid kit. And, John, phone for a doctor.'

'I don't need a doc –' began Evans urgently, waving one brown hand.

'Now, now,' broke in Mrs Hodge. 'You need medical treatment. Our house is just round the corner. I'll bathe and bandage your leg so that with any luck you can struggle to the house and be in bed for the doctor.'

Evans seemed more relaxed. 'Thank you,' he breathed, as John headed back to the house, his golden hair ruffled in the breeze.

'There's a stream near here,' Mrs Hodge said as she delved into the picnic basket and transferred some sandwiches from a plastic picnic box into a paper bag. 'Do you know it, Michelle?'

'No, sorry.'

'Well, I'll go then. I'm going to fill this sandwich box with water to wash Mr Evans's leg. Stay with him, Michelle, and see he's all right.' The stout woman hurried away.

Michelle poured Evans some more juice, found a swimming-towel for him to wipe his face with, helped him out of his anorak, and handed him her comb because his strands of dark hair kept slipping over his face. While he gulped down the juice, spilling it down his rough chin, Michelle took in his features. There was no twinkle in his eyes, which were set deeply under a protruding brow bearing permanent frown lines. Whiskers of a beard speckled his wide lower jaw and his thin lips were twisted downwards. The face was rough, quite tanned, pitted with a few dents and had a strained look about it. Evans spoke a little as he tugged at his grimy, matted hair with the comb.

'You're Michelle?'

'Yes, Michelle Ward.'

'I'm – er – sorry if I'm a bother.'

'Of course not!' Michelle said in admonishing tones. The towel gained a criss-cross design of smudged dirt streaks as Evans wiped his sweat-coated face. There was an awkward silence, so Michelle hastily changed the subject.

'Have you written any other books?'

'Books? Oh, books!' Yes – no! I mean I have written one but it didn't get published.'

'What was it called?'

'Er –' Evans buried his hot face in the towel. '*British Waterside Plants*,' he replied when he had wiped his face.

'How interesting,' Michelle exclaimed. 'What are you going to do when you reach the Highlands?'

'What am I going to do? Er . . .'

'I mean how are you going to study flowers?'

'Well, I look at them through magnifying glasses and em . . . photograph them, you see –'

'And make notes?'

'Yes, and make notes.'

'Do you have to carry your camera and note-books with you all the time, then?'

'Er – yes.'

'In your rucksack?'

'Er – yes.'

Michelle glanced at the rucksack, smeared with filth, on the motorbike near by. 'I do hope the camera didn't get broken during your accident.'

'It didn't,' Evans said hurriedly, folding up the towel. 'I looked.'

'Would you like me to check for you?'

'No, no, it's quite all right,' he said, smoothing back his hair.

'Could I have a look at your notes and the begin-ning of the book? I'm very interested in nature.' Michelle had already crossed to the rucksack.

'I'd rather you didn't,' Evans said calmly. 'You see, I like to keep all my notes secret, so no one has read the book before it's finished.'

'I see. It doesn't matter. I was just interested,' Michelle explained, but something had caught her eye. Sewn on to the neck of the rucksack was a tiny label bearing the name P. N. Sewell.

'It is *your* rucksack, isn't it?' she blurted out.

'Of course.' He sounded annoyed. 'Whose did you think it was?'

As Michelle stuttered in embarrassment, Mrs

Hodge arrived back and placed the plastic box full of swirling water on the ground. With another swimming-towel she began to bathe Evans's wound. As she washed it the water turned to a sickening red with gravel floating about in it.

Panting hard, John came back on the scene with flushed cheeks.

'Dr Barlow's coming – soon as he can – in an hour or so,' he announced, opening up the first-aid kit. While Mrs Hodge was tearing up cotton-wool and trying to remove all the gravel from the wound, Michelle surreptitiously pointed out to John the label on Evans's rucksack. John gave a puzzled frown and shrugged.

'I need more water,' Mrs Hodge said, handing Michelle the container of gruesome liquid. 'See if you can find the stream.' She gave some directions. Michelle set off to the distant trees. But after a while she came running back, calling that she could not find the stream. Mrs Hodge gave an exasperated sigh and went to show Michelle the way. John, left alone with Evans, began an amiable conversation about motorbikes. He stopped abruptly when he heard a yell from Mrs Hodge carried on the wind. John sprang to his feet and addressed Evans apologetically.

'I'm sorry, but I'll have to leave you for a moment. Something may have happened to Mrs Hodge. Will you be all right?'

Evans nodded and John hurried off anxiously. Evans propped himself up against the tree in a more comfortable position. He stared aimlessly at

17

the meandering road which stretched over the uneven land as far as his eye could see. Suddenly, far,
far away on the horizon, a grey-silver speck
appeared on the road and glinted in the sunlight.
It wound its way along, gradually becoming clearer
and larger. Evans stiffened. Eyes widening, he
peered at the silver car, with a rigid back and limbs.
He struggled to his feet, clutching the lean tree
trunk. He discovered his leg was causing him less
pain. He reached out with shaking hands for his
rucksack. His trembling fingers fumbled with the
neck of it. Evans tried to calm himself. 'It might
not be them,' he muttered reassuringly to himself,
but becoming all the more nervous. With fear flickering in his eyes and his heart quivering, he delved
into the rucksack, plunging his hand between cloth
and boxes. His sweating fingertips touched cool
metal and he tugged out a pair of binoculars. The
fumbling had cost him only a few seconds, but lost
time, however short, could mean a lot to Evans. He
had to steady himself before he could hold the
binoculars to his eyes without them shaking up and
down. The silver car was still at a distance.
Through the binoculars he could see it winding
along the gravel road – slowly because of the nu-
merous bumps and dips in the ground. Evans swallowed hard. Yes, the car *was* a Mercedes-Benz, and
there were several dark, hefty figures in it. Evans
could feel his hair prickling on his sticky scalp. It
took him an effort to move himself; for seconds he
just stood there, his whiskered face a sickly grey.
But another glance at the approaching car caused

18

him to step back to his motorbike. He shoved the binoculars back into the rucksack and snatched up his anorak. The sudden dashing about aggravated his leg-wound, which started stinging and aching. The permanent frown lines on his forehead deepened. He glanced around nervously. The two withering trees behind him would not hide him. The wood John had just headed for was too far for Evans to struggle to in time. He would have to escape on his motorbike before they saw him.

He was so frightened and engrossed in the car that he had not noticed the return of the cousins and Mrs Hodge. The latter had yelled because she had tripped over a tree root, but was not hurt. Now they had fetched the water and were surprised to see Evans on his feet.

'*Mr Evans!*' exclaimed Mrs Hodge, as he began to wheel his motorbike to the roadside. 'What are you doing? Where –?'

'I'm sorry, Mrs Hodge,' Evans burbled, as he painfully swung his leg over the saddle, 'But I must be going. I –' Mrs Hodge's restraining hand came down on his shoulder like a ton of bricks.

'You're going to see a doctor.'

Evans lifted his ashen face. His choking breaths revealed his terror, as he shook his head uneasily.

'No, no.' He shrugged Mrs Hodge's hand off his shoulder with a frightened glance at the still distant Mercedes. Suddenly an idea sprang into his head.

'Mr Evans, where are you going?' began Michelle.

'You wouldn't be so crazy as to attempt to ride

19

your bike with that leg?' chimed in John, with a slight tone of annoyance in his voice. But Evans was digging into his rucksack. Mrs Hodge tried again.

'If you would kindly explain what –' but Evans, having pulled a matchbox from his rucksack, turned to them and interrupted with a very hasty speech.

'You've all been so kind to me.' He shoved the matchbox into Michelle's hands. 'Accept this as a token of my gratitude. I – I can't stay here any longer. You see – I – er –' but there was no time to think up an excuse. A glance at the approaching Mercedes-Benz made him forget his speech. He wondered if he had done the right thing, giving Michelle the precious matchbox. But it was too late to change his mind now. It would be safe with Michelle. Who would expect a young girl to have it? And, Evans reminded himself, he was coming back to steal it when he had given the silver car the slip. The motorbike engine coughed and spluttered, then broke into a steady hum. Evans drove it along the road with John, Michelle and Mrs Hodge dashing after him. The motorbike sped away in a pother of dust; shortly afterwards the silver Mercedes zoomed past in a flash.

The cousins and Mrs Hodge were utterly mystified as they stood at the roadside.

'Shall we go after him?' asked the impetuous John.

'No, it's not really our business where he's going,'

Michelle reminded them. 'We wouldn't catch him now anyway.'

'No. I doubt if my ancient Fiat would match the speed of his bike,' Mrs Hodge observed. 'Let him go where he wants, ungrateful man that he is!'

'He must be mad – pure mad,' added John, 'giving us a box of matches.'

'It's not,' Michelle told him, opening the box. She raised her eyebrows. 'How kind of him!'

'*Kind*!' blustered John, not realising what was in the box.

'Look here.' Michelle showed them a small silver heart-shaped locket on a chain with some pretty yet unusual engraving on the front.

'Oh!' Mrs Hodge's mood changed. 'Is there anything in it?'

'No,' replied Michelle. 'But if you ask me, he must have had a good reason for dashing off like that – a very good reason, and it was very thoughtful of him to give us this.' Little did she realise Evans's evil intention to return and steal the locket back.

John's anger was appeased. 'I wish I knew what his reason was,' he murmured curiously. 'It's all quite exciting.'

'We must go home,' piped up Mrs Hodge, 'and phone Dr Barlow to explain what's happened. I only hope that he hasn't set off already,'

'Yes,' observed John. 'It wouldn't have been much use carrying on with this picnic anyway. Everything's covered in blood and grit. I'm going to carry on making my model aeroplane and listen to my radio when we get home.'

'No, we're not staying indoors on a day like this,' Michelle refused. 'We'll wash the things and set off again.'

'Yes,' agreed Mrs Hodge, who was determined to gain a sun-tan to rival the cousins'. 'It won't take a minute to repack, and it's a beautiful day.'

It was not long before they were on their way back to the beach, John having collected his old cricket bat and ball in the hope of practising his googlies. The sunlight streaked the land and wild roses reached out their pretty pink heads to drink in the light. Any wispy coils of clouds were drifting away, leaving a sky as blue as the delicate petals of a forget-me-not. When they reached the sea its surface was shimmering with glinting golden ripples, the sand was as smooth as if it had been painted on the ground and the rocks were sun-scorched. Mrs Hodge settled down with her back against a rock to read while the cousins waded into the warm water and struck out for a tiny island, which was sucking hot sunlight into its rock surface and cast a cool shadow on the water. Both being strong swimmers, it didn't take long before they were stretched out on the hot rock island with water running off them and forming a maze of tiny pools.

'I'm glad we came out,' admitted John. 'This is the best summer we've had for years. I'm enjoying myself.'

'Even without your radio?'

John laughed. 'Yes, even without that. You talk as if I spend half my life with it.'

'The understatement of the year!' cried Michelle. '*Half* your life? I'd say ninety-nine point nine nine percent of it.'

'Come off it,' John smiled, lifting his face to the sun to bask in its gorgeous heat. 'There are a lot of good groups around now.'

'Or a lot of pretty girls?' Michelle's eyes sparkled mischievously as she stretched out lazily.

'What's *that* supposed to mean?' demanded John, sitting bolt upright with a curious smile.

'Well, you seem to go for all the groups with pretty girls in them, especially blondes,' grinned Michelle knowingly.

John's eyes widened in strong indignation. 'Balderdash!' he exclaimed and promptly rattled through a long list of all-male groups he liked. 'Besides,' he ended, his voice lowering, 'I prefer girls with hazel eyes and long chestnut hair who come swimming with me –'

Michelle squirmed in embarrassment. John was sitting dangerously close to the edge of the tiny island. One push would send him flying into the water and Michelle provided that push. In went John and up went a spray of sparkling water. As the boy surfaced, coughing and spluttering, and vowing revenge, Michelle dived in and, grinning, headed for the beach at top speed, followed by John. She reached it a whisker ahead of him and ran over the sand, leaving wet footprints and giggling at her success in ducking her cousin.

'You'll regret this,' promised John, striding across the beach; he was trying to look angry but couldn't stop a grin creeping over his face as he reached for a towel.

'I thought it was too good to be true,' observed Michelle, seeing John picking up his radio during the picnic later on.

'What's too good to be true?'

'You leaving that thing off. Still, I should've known you couldn't live much longer without putting it on.'

'I just want to hear how the Test at Headingley is going.'

'Oh! We're not going to have an endless cricket commentary inflicted on us while we eat, are we?' begged Michelle. But it was no use. As John chewed away on an egg sandwich, the transistor was in its usual place, by his ear, and he would mutter now and then comments such as, 'Three hundred and fifteen for eight. Could have been worse!' or cry triumphantly, 'Bowled 'im!' He was the sporting type for, besides cricket, he enjoyed tennis, soccer and swimming. Had his father let him have his way, his bedroom would have had, instead of wallpaper, posters of pop and sporting idols.

After the picnic the cousins went for a long walk through woods and along clifftops, discussing topics ranging from the films John's father had made to their teachers and schoolfriends and Mrs Hodge's firm rule that if either of the cousins squeezed the toothpaste from the middle of the tube they could go out and buy their own! It grew cooler and Michelle was glad she had brought a light cardigan with her. The hours drifted away and, as the sun sank a little, clouds gathered on the horizon, some of them forming shapes recognisable as a human profile or as a dog's silhouette. As purple shadows crept over the beach the cousins started a game of cricket, using a rock as a wicket, but this ended when John hit a six into the sea a long way out and the hard rubber ball was carried away on the water. Mrs Hodge, now red from the sun, said it was time she made supper, so they set off back to the cottage.

During supper John switched on his radio again. The local news was on. Suddenly all three stiffened, their faces full of alarm, as the voice on the radio said,

'A body has been found in the sea on the south-west Scottish coast near Ballantrae by some picnickers. The body has not been identified, though it was a man in his middle-thirties dressed in a brown anorak with grey shirt and trousers. It seems that the man fell over the cliff as a damaged motorbike was overturned at the roadside near the cliff edge' – at this Mrs Hodge and the cousins gasped in dismay – 'but the police say that foul play has not been ruled out. They are eager to contact anyone who can give any information . . .'

chapter two

A Shock In The Night

As the radio blared away giving more details, all three stared at one another horror-stricken. The name Evans was running through their heads. The subject on the radio changed to sport. John flicked off the transistor impatiently and took in a deep breath. Michelle sat open-mouthed. Mrs Hodge sucked in her lips and was first to break the deathly hush.

'Do you think it was?'

'Most probably,' John reluctantly admitted, staring at his shoes.

'It's horrible to think about,' declared Michelle with a shiver. 'It must have been his leg – he couldn't have ridden properly with it.'

'Maybe it wasn't an accident,' murmured John, mainly to himself, but in a voice audible to Mrs Hodge and Michelle. The latter bit her lip.

'John, don't say that,' she whispered, and suddenly she remembered the silver car racing after Evans's motorbike and wondered . . .

Mrs Hodge slowly rose to her feet and began to stack the dishes.

'I'll phone the police and tell them we have information to give,' she proposed.

'We don't know it was Evans,' Michelle protested.

'All the details fit,' John said.

'Yes, you're right. It's just that I was desperately hoping it wasn't. Silly of me I suppose.'

'In any case we must give the police our information,' decided Mrs Hodge. 'John, you know more about the motorbike.'

'Yes. And the number-plate – I think it had an L and an N on it – and maybe a four,' John said, his brow furrowed with concentration.

'Write down all the details of it,' Mrs Hodge suggested. 'If the description fits, then it's almost positively Mr Evans who – who was riding it.'

John nodded and rose. While he fetched paper and pencil, Michelle retired to her room and sank on to her bed, remembering with regret the black thoughts she had had of Evans when he had driven off.

At last the patient Mrs Hodge got through to Sergeant Blakely on the telephone. Blakely had been helping to investigate the incident and was eager to hear someone willing to relate information. Mrs Hodge explained their suspicions and read out the notes John had made. John watched from the kitchen doorway as Mrs Hodge nodded, listened and spoke to the Sergeant with a strained, wretched expression dominating her countenance. The phone tinkled as she put down the receiver and approached John.

'They told me a lot.' She swallowed hard. 'It was Mr Evans all right. I told them all we know. A

man's coming here tonight to question us. Oh –
and the rucksack was missing from the motorbike.
Strange that. It was definitely Mr Evans's bike,
though.'

'Hmm.' John looked thoughtful. He went up to
Michelle's room. She was slouched on the bed, her
eyes hot and painful with trying to keep back tears
as she fingered the silver locket which was misty
from the condensation from her sweating fingers.
After breaking the news, John sat down beside her,
realising how she felt. Eventually he held out his
hand.

'May I see it?' he asked gently, indicating the
locket.

As he toyed with it Michelle asked cautiously,
'Was it my imagination or did *you* see a silver car
flash past after Evans left?'

'I saw it.' John swung the locket from side to
side on its chain.

'It – it was going pretty fast, wasn't it?'

'Like you say, pretty fast.'

'It was going after Evans's motorbike.'

John dropped the locket on the bed between
them. 'Well, I – don't know. I've been thinking –
maybe Evans saw the car coming and that's why
he left so suddenly. When he had gone a short
distance with the car after him, then – no – it's
absurd – I don't want to upset you.'

'It's all right. I know what you were going to
say. You think that whoever was in the car might
have – er – thrown Evans off the cliff. It's possible,
but why?'

'I've no idea. Oh, really!' exclaimed John. 'How stupid we are, making up murder stories. It was a plain accident. I must be nuts.'

The shrill sound of the doorbell pierced the stillness of the house. The cousins trooped down to the living-room to be introduced to Inspector Davis, a tall individual with bony white cheeks and contrasting black tufty hair, and another man called Burton, who, plump and red-faced with thinning hair, was bursting out of his blue uniform, and seemed very hot and utterly fed up. He hardly spoke at all but sat staring at the stern and serious Inspector Davis, who sat very upright in his chair, drilling out formal questions. However, at some of the cousins' answers he seemed quietly interested and his stony expression perhaps melted ever so slightly as he raised his eyebrows and enquired, 'A Mercedes-Benz possibly chasing this Evans, eh? Hear that, Burton?'

A vaguely interested grunt emerged from the sprawled out mass in an armchair.

'Of course, we could be wrong, but it did look suspicious,' chimed in Mrs Hodge, glancing uneasily at the massive Burton and hoping the chair would hold out.

'Interesting,' muttered the Inspector, stroking his chin. 'You see, around the spot where the motorbike had overturned there were tyre tracks and possibly signs of a struggle.'

Michelle swallowed hard and John pursed his lips uneasily. 'D'you really think so?'

'We do indeed.'

While Davis made some notes Michelle fetched the locket she had mentioned earlier. The Inspector turned it over in his hand and nodded.

'Yes, very pretty. That's a very nice – well – thank you gift. This Evans doesn't sound a bad chap. We don't seem to have any records on him.'

'Try looking under the name of Sewell,' suggested Michelle. Davis looked at her enquiringly and she explained about the name-tag on Evans's rucksack. The Inspector pointed out that it could have been borrowed, but promised he would look into it. The cousins and Mrs Hodge did not find the interview particularly enjoyable. It depressed them to talk about Evans and, besides, they were all very weary. At last the policeman left, thanking them formally. As Mrs Hodge returned to the kitchen, Michelle turned to John.

'Let's take our minds off this. Why don't you provide me with some comic relief by playing – *trying* to play your clarinet?' she suggested, grinning.

John laughed. He had made it his duty to let everyone who was aware that he played the instrument know that he was hopeless at it. All the same he retired to his room and promptly massacred 'Georgia On My Mind'. Recovering from hysterics Michelle described it as 'different'.

'Let's go and watch television,' suggested John, as he cleaned out the instrument which had crushed Mr Lester's hopes of his son becoming a talented musician. 'There's a good film on.' They watched this for the rest of the evening.

As the sun set and pink and violet streaks stained

the sky, Michelle climbed into bed. It was a hot, stuffy night – one of those nights when you lie in bed with sheets sticking to your body. Michelle had flung open the windows and wrenched the blankets off her bed, but still she lay sweating. Hours passed as her clock ticked away. She fell into a groggy half-sleep. About one o'clock in the morning she woke again. The heat was too much. Michelle flung off her sheet and paced round the room. She went into the bathroom and took a drink of water. As she crossed the landing she heard a low voice downstairs. Who was up? John? Well, it couldn't be Mrs Hodge; she took sleeping-pills. Then who was John talking to? Again a voice drifted up the stairs, but Michelle could not identify it. She cautiously descended the stairs, peering over the banisters, but the light was too dim to perceive anyone. Why hadn't John switched on a lamp? Michelle reached the hall. Again she heard a voice – a man's voice. The girl stopped in her tracks, puzzled and momentarily struck with fear. Could it be burglars? But why would anyone bother to come all the way to *this* house, which was far from any village and had nothing really valuable in it? A cloud uncovered the moon and a beam of silvery light stretched across the hall through the thin muslin curtains at the window. Michelle was sure the voices were coming from the lounge. She boldly crept to the half open door and peeped round. A board creaked as she did so but so quietly that she hoped no one had heard it. However, as she peered into the dark room, she thought she heard a click, and a cold

31

chill of fear filled her as the low voices stopped abruptly. Unknown to her, the click had been a torch being flicked off. She could see nothing in the dark room and was about to back into the hall nervously when someone pulled her into the room and hastily closed the door. As Michelle sucked in her breath to scream, half shaking with shock, a clammy hand was clapped over her mouth and her arms were pinned behind her back. A split second later she was blinded by the dazzling beam of a torch being shot at her eyes. The girl struggled furiously and when the torch beam was swung away she saw a slim, sandy-haired man who crossed the room to help pin back her flailing arms with a grip like iron. During her persistent struggling she caught a glimpse of her assailants over her shoulder. The first man was broad-shouldered with thinning hair and a grim face. He was also, Michelle noted, annoyingly strong. There were three other men in the room watching, one holding the torch. Exhaustion and the unwelcome sight of these other men caused the frightened Michelle to give up her struggling.

'It's not the boy,' grumbled the dark-haired man holding the torch.

'Shurrup, Sanders!' snarled the even rougher-looking thug at his side. 'We'll soon find out what we want to know from her.'

For the first time, Michelle noticed the state of the room. Drawers had been opened and rifled and the bureau was forced open, its contents scattered on the table and floor.

'OK. Get going, Hackett,' Sanders said. 'We 'aven't got all night.' The hefty Hackett approached Michelle, staring through piercing slit-shaped eyes. His lower jaw was squarish, his upper lip slightly twisted in a menacing manner. Michelle writhed uneasily in the unweakening hold of the sandy-haired man and his broad-shouldered mate. The cruel, forbidding look on Hackett's face made her heart pound against her ribs as if it wanted to break out.

'You can be quite useful to us,' sneered Hackett. 'First – this.' He held up a scrapbook belonging to John which they must have found in the bureau. John had brought it on holiday to show to Michelle because it contained all the newspaper cuttings about his actor father. Above the cuttings, which were neatly pasted into the book, John had written things such as 'Dad at Alvington Theatre, Feb. 17th'. John's name was printed on the front of the book and Hackett prodded a finger at it.

'If,' he said, 'my deductions are correct, this belongs to the son of the actor, Gareth Lester. He's been in the news a lot lately – must have been making quite a bit of cash – yeh – *quite* a bit.'

Reading his thoughts, Michelle glared, scared and angry.

'So John Lester is in this house,' continued Hackett, as if there was no doubt that his deductions were correct. 'An' who are *you*? What've you got to do with John Lester? OK, you can let her talk, Dudgeon, but listen, girl, Sanders here is a tough

'un. Don't try anything funny. Sanders has a gun
– so have I.' He looked threatening. Dudgeon uncovered Michelle's mouth. For a moment her lips
trembled. Then, trying to keep her voice steady,
she told them, 'I'm a relation of John's – a cousin.
He isn't here. I'm sorry to disappoint you but he's
gone – gone – er – on location with his dad, who's
making a film. The scrapbook – er – well, he left
that for me.' She had to lie for the sake of John's
safety. Hastily she added sceptically, 'And the guns
– *if* you've got any – well, if you use them, all the
people in the house will be woken up and you'll be
up to your eyes in trouble.'

But her voice quavered slightly and her bold
words must have lacked conviction because, after
Dudgeon had covered up her mouth again, Hackett
sneered, 'Never you mind the guns. If you try to
scream or anything, we have other ways of dealing
with troublemakers. And as for that rubbish about
John being away, don't you try double-crossing me.
D'you think I can't see when you're making up
tales in your head? I'm warning you, don't try
being smart. That boy's in this house and you're
trying to hide it. As for you being his cousin – well,
that's one thing I might believe. But you're not
going to lie to *this* question. OK?' His eyes flashed
angrily and his fierce voice scared Michelle. She
was also worried for John, who was blissfully un-
aware of all that was going on. Sanders stepped
into the pool of light cast by the torch and squared
his shoulders.

'I'll deal with her if she makes a noise,' he mut-

34

tered. Michelle desperately wished it was all a bad dream but everything was too unbearably real.

'The question,' went on Hackett, 'is this. The locket – where is it? The silver locket. You know what I mean. OK, Dudgeon, let her talk.' What was the use of another lie, Michelle thought? Perhaps, she hoped fervently, they would clear out if they had the locket. Never mind what they wanted it for.

'It's in my room,' she told them, 'opposite the top of the stairs. Look in the chest of drawers, third drawer down – em – left side.'

'OK,' Hackett nodded. 'Coker' – to the fifth member of the gang, a bewildered-looking man in a raincoat – 'get it and make it snappy.'

'What about getting the boy?' enquired Coker dopily.

'Get the locket first,' Hackett told him. 'I'll have to think about this a bit. There could be a lot of money involved. The girl might be worth a bit too, *if* she's his cousin. OK, Coker – *get the locket* and bring it back here. We'll take the girl to the car and come back for the boy.'

Michelle was going to squeal, 'You can't do this,' but didn't think she would be able to keep her voice steady. Then she suddenly realised that Dudgeon hadn't covered up her mouth again. It was her only chance! She had to do something. She couldn't let them do this!

'*Johhhhn*!' she shrieked. The four remaining men started. Dudgeon hurriedly clasped his hand over Michelle's mouth as Hackett's face clouded over with fury. Simultaneously Sanders stepped forward and dealt Michelle a blow on the side of her head. Her knees buckled and she blacked out.

John woke with a start. A scream had invaded his peaceful dreams. Or had he dreamt the scream? Someone had shrieked his name. He sat up in bed, alarmed. It could have been a nightmare but, all the same, he climbed out of bed. He walked on to the landing. Michelle's bedroom door was open and her bed empty . . . His heart jumped, but then he realised that she had probably wanted a drink of water in the hot night. He entered the bathroom but she was not there. When he came back on to the landing he caught sight of a figure hurrying down the stairs. It was too hefty a figure to be Michelle. 'Burglars?' thought John. If so Michelle could be in danger! He scurried barefooted after the figure. Was it Michelle who had screamed? It had sounded like a female scream. When he reached the hall he found, to his astonishment, the front door open. He was just wondering if he should phone the police when he saw two figures carrying a girl in a white nightdress across the lawn. John's lower jaw dropped. Forgetting fear, danger and common sense, he leapt through the front door and tore across the lawn. He caught hold of one man's ankle, so that he tumbled to the ground, letting go of Michelle's legs. John pounced on the man and sat on him, legs astride, yelling, 'What d'you think you're doing, you great brute?'

Dudgeon was astonished. He tried to push John off him. Rumsey, the sandy-haired man, dumped

Michelle by some bushes and rushed to Dudgeon's assistance. He arrived there before Hackett, Sanders and Coker and, putting his arms round John's waist, tried to tug off the boy. But John's fists clung to the lapels of Dudgeon's jacket. Dudgeon's nostrils widened. He snorted like a horse and sweat broke out on his forehead.

John yelled wildly, 'You dirty crooks! You won't get away with this. How dare you lay hands on my cousin? I'll get the police on to you. You'll be sorry! Bullies, brutes . . .'

Rumsey still tried to tug him off. John grimly hung on, but realised he was outnumbered.

'So it's the boy!' Sanders's voice came through the darkness. 'Ain't he a little spitfire?'

'Get off me, you pest!' hissed Dudgeon through gritted teeth. Sanders seized John's arm and dragged him on to the lawn. Dudgeon sprang to his feet, seething with anger and brushing dust and soil from his coat. John fought like a tiger. Sanders's fist lashed out – pain flared up in the side of John's head and he sank into a terrifying black emptiness.

chapter three

Hackett's Hideout

Groaning, John tried to open his eyes. His head was buzzing and he was aware of pressure on either side of him. Dizzy and weak, he tried to figure out where he was. The night's events came back to him in a flash. So where was he now? What time was it? And Michelle – where was she? Struck with anxiety, John perceived through half open eyes the shadowy figures of the men. He distinguished bright beams of light tunnelling through the inky blackness and began to recognise the burr of a car engine; he knew he must be in the back of a vehicle, squashed between the men. Everything before him in the car was blurred and dark and he couldn't see Michelle. He felt very weak and unable to move. Worry was mixed with his discomfort. Had they got Michelle or left her in the garden tied up or . . . dead!

John broke into a cold sweat and with difficulty moved his dry, cracked lips. He was breathing heavily.

'Wh – where i-s m-my c-cousi-n?' he murmured, choking on the words.

'She's OK,' sneered Hackett's drawling voice. 'At least she will be if you keep your mouth shut and don't make trouble.' John was not feeling fit enough to make trouble even if he had wanted to.

'Wh – what – where is she?' he breathed.

'In the car, flat out. Now shut up,' Sanders's voice snapped at his ear. With an ache hammering on the inside of his head, John tried to see her. It was a strain to swivel his eyes; his head fell forward and he half fainted into a deep, hot sleep.

John's eyes flickered open but everything before him was hazy. He breathed heavily in and out. His head ached dreadfully. The picture before his eyes grew clearer and he realised he was lying down. Slowly and giddily he propped himself up on one elbow. He was in a room which smelt unpleasantly of alcohol and cigarette smoke. Next to him lay Michelle, not fully conscious. There was a nasty bruise on one side of her forehead. John could feel one stinging on his forehead also. It made him wince to touch it. Through a haze of cigarette smoke he could see Hackett and Sanders playing cards. Hackett was scowling as he flung his last card on the table. Sanders grinned and tucked several crinkled notes inside his jacket. Hackett turned a stony gaze on John, who looked to the other side of the room. Rumsey was slouched on a moth-eaten settee with beer running down his bristled chin, and three empty cans littered the floor. Coker was engrossed in a football magazine while Dudgeon smoked peacefully with two ashtrays packed with cigarette stubs on the table beside him. He became aware of John watching him, and glowered from under thick, bushy eyebrows.

'Hackett, the boy's woke up,' Dudgeon said.

'I know,' was the gruff reply. 'So what? Wait till the girl's better too.' He turned back to Sanders and began to deal out the cards afresh. There was a crack and a hiss as Rumsey opened another can of beer. The drink sloshed into the glass and Rumsey slurped it down greedily. John glanced round the room. There was no window but a bare bulb swung from the ceiling. The walls were cracked and the plaster was peeling off and hanging down in strips. The floor, where John was lying, was boarded, with worn mats here and there. A radiator, rusty where paint had been scratched off, stretched along one wall. The furniture was sparse: two tables, six chairs, the settee, a telephone, two filthy mattresses in a corner with a heap of blankets piled on them and a new, sparkling clean white fridge which looked very out of place and made all the other things look even dirtier than they actually were. There were two doors, one with a lock and bolts on the inside, the other open revealing a tiny washroom with a sink and lavatory.

Michelle gave a grunt. Slowly and painfully she regained full consciousness. Hackett, who was losing his game again, and glad of an excuse to stop, strode over to the cousins. Coker put down his magazine; he and Dudgeon looked on. As Hackett opened his mouth to speak, the drunken Rumsey broke into a tuneless song, swaying back and forth and clutching his beer mug.

'Aw, shurrup,' bawled Hackett. Rumsey sniggered drunkenly. The cousins sat up and leaned against the wall. Hackett took the silver locket from his pocket and swung it centimetres from Michelle's face.

'Least you told us correctly where this was,' he said to her. 'Didn't do very well after that, though, did you? Screaming like that.' Michelle pursed her lips.

'Nah,' agreed Sanders, his dark eyes twinkling as he watched from his seat.

'What do you want with it anyhow?' demanded John, stretching his stiff arms, 'and – and how did you know *we'd* got it?'

None of the men answered. The same thought crossed each cousin's mind. Evans was the only one who knew that Michelle had the locket. The men must have forced him to tell them. The silver car . . . Evans's death . . . the unwelcome answer was staring them in the face. Hackett and his men must have been in that car and, after learning where the locket was, they must have . . . pushed Evans off the cliff. The idea was horrible, but it was the obvious solution. And this meant the cousins were with murderers! A glance at each other proved they both realised this.

'Anyway, what do you want with us now?' burst in Michelle. 'You've got the locket.'

'Ah, well.' Hackett grinned evilly as he nodded at John. 'This wise guy here is son of Gareth Lester.' John stiffened angrily. 'And,' went on Hackett, 'this Gareth Lester – well, he ain't exactly huntin' in the gutter for his dinner. Anyone c'n see that from the house you were in. All swish furniture. We've read 'bout your dad, you know. Lives in Leicester. Got money. Yeh, *lots* of money. We figured we'd get a nice packet fer – er – borrowing 'is son – and 'is niece. What d'you think?'

'I think you're balmy!' John burst out angrily. 'I think you ought to jolly well –'

'Don't try being smart, son. We don't like cheeky guys, do we, Sanders?'

'Nah,' agreed Sanders. ' 'Ow much d'ye reckon, Hackett?'

'Bin thinking,' announced Hackett. 'Fifty thousand.' John and Michelle exchanged horrified glances.

'You mean pounds?' gulped Michelle.

'My dad's not a millionaire, you know,' John said with incredulous eyes. 'There's no way – *no way* – he can afford that preposterous amount and you must know it.'

Hackett laughed wryly. 'Bah! That holiday cottage you were in is worth plenty. If your dad can't cough up the rest he must be in a bad way.'

John's eyes flashed angrily. 'Don't be stupid! We can't sell the holiday cottage –'

'Why not? You've got a proper 'ouse in Leicester.'

'But –'

'Tell the kid to shurrup, Hackett,' burst in an agitated Sanders. 'You better phone the Tigress 'bout this.'

'Who's that?' enquired Michelle.

42

'Never you mind,' Hackett replied sharply yet a trifle smugly; then he addressed Sanders and remarked contemptuously, 'I intend to.'

Rumsey suddenly rolled off the sofa on to the floor, giggling and drooling.

'Aw, for Pete's sake,' blustered Hackett. 'Sober up that loony.' Dudgeon stubbed out his cigarette and dragged Rumsey into the washroom. He filled the basin with cold water and ducked Rumsey's head four times. Rumsey yelled and spluttered in protest. Calmly, Dudgeon returned to his seat and opened another packet of cigarettes. Rumsey staggered back to the settee, coughing and spluttering, blinking water out of his eyes and shaking his wet hair about. The beads of water trickled down his denim jacket.

Hackett shot Rumsey a disgusted look and turned to Sanders.

'You seem to have forgotten, ole feller, Tigress said not ter phone till after one. She's out on a job – remember?' Sanders grunted, annoyed at his mistake.

'What's so special about that locket anyway?' Michelle asked Hackett.

'Wouldn't you like to know?' Hackett obviously took a great deal of pleasure out of being one step ahead of everyone.

'It's very valuable?' suggested Michelle.

'No.' Hackett slipped it back into his pocket. 'At least, not in money. It's valuable for something else.'

'You can't get away with this,' piped up John. 'The police are bound to –'

'Look, kid!' snapped Hackett. 'I'm a bit sick of you. You'd better watch it. You and the girl change and then keep quiet.

'Change into what?'

'Coker fetched your clothes last night.' With this Hackett stomped to the fridge, poured out some lager and slouched down at the table to drink it.

Coker handed the cousins their clothes which he had picked up from the chairs in their bedrooms the night before.

'You can change in there one by one,' said Sanders, indicating the washroom.

'Thanks.' Michelle found Sanders a slightly pleasanter character than Hackett. He was even quite handsome with his glossy dark hair and twinkling eyes, though his face was harsh.

John changed first. He came out of the washroom wearing jeans, and pulling a brown jersey on over his shirt. He glanced at Coker.

'You forgot one of my socks,' he declared. Sanders couldn't stifle a snigger at John's tone of disgust.

'Too bad,' Coker grinned. 'I remembered your watch, though.' John held out his hand. 'But' – added Coker tauntingly – 'I decided it was too expensive for a youngster like you, so I may as well do you the favour of keeping it myself.' Coker's smug grin infuriated John. He gave Coker a very black look and walked past him with dignity.

When Michelle was changed they discovered that it was 11.15 a.m. Hackett finished his lager and settled back to do the crossword in an old newspaper. The other men knew very well not to disturb him when he was in a sullen, silent mood. The cousins spent an unpleasant hour worrying. John's parents would stop their cruise, while Mr and Mrs Ward would come back from France. Their holidays would be spoiled. Mrs Hodge would be worried sick. They both had a deep dread of what would become of them.

At noon Sanders looked in the fridge.

'Not much,' he announced. 'Coker, go and get some fish and chips.'

Coker sighed and flung down his magazine.

'Why me?' Sanders glared at him. 'OK, OK, but I'll need some cash.' Sanders stuffed three notes into Coker's grubby hand.

'Better bring an extra portion for the kids,' he snapped. 'Get going! For Pete's sake, you don't need that raincoat!'

Coker ignored the remark. 'Key.'

Sanders delved into his pocket and tossed Coker a key. The lock clicked and Coker drew back the bolt. He threw the key back to Sanders, who re-locked the door when Coker had left. When Coker opened the door the cousins caught sight of some banisters opposite but then the door closed.

Coker returned in about half an hour. He flung an early edition of an evening newspaper on to the couch and dumped a packet of fish meals on the table. The odour was delicious. Sanders dealt out the packets of crisp golden haddock. The cousins shared one between them. Hackett and Rumsey ate like pigs, munching with their mouths open and spitting out the bones.

After lunch Hackett snatched up the newspaper Coker had bought and turned to the sports page. He swore.

'What's up?' enquired Dudgeon.

'Johnny Roberts has asked for a transfer, that's what!' Hackett snapped.

'I wouldn't call that much of a loss,' piped up John. 'He's hopeless. All he can do with the ball is to kick it into the crowd.'

In a fit of anger Hackett flung the paper at him violently. John calmly picked it up and suddenly caught sight of a familiar face in it – his own!

'By gum!' John exclaimed. 'Michelle, there's something about us being missing here!'

'What!' snapped Hackett. He snatched the paper, tearing a page down the middle as he did so. Sanders peered over Hackett's shoulder.

'Says Lester's coming back from a cruise with his wife. Won't be back yet, so it's no use phoning 'em for a bit.'

'Hmmm.' Hackett stroked his chin. 'I guess we could send a note an' phone later.'

Sanders opened his mouth to speak but John broke in, enraged.

'See what you've done! My parents were going to enjoy that cruise and you've spoilt it! Now they'll spend their holidays sitting at home worrying!' His fists were clenched at his sides and he was appealing to Sanders, but Hackett rounded on him fiercely.

'Won't have to worry as long as they get that ransom –'

'Which they can't!'

'Will you shurrup!' Hackett looked so fierce that Michelle was frightened for John. Sanders glanced at his watch and laid a hand on Hackett's arm, turning him round.

'Time you phoned the Tigress.'

'OK.' Hackett nodded. 'I 'aven't forgotten.' Hackett flung himself on to the settee and snatched up the black receiver. His sausage-like finger dialled a number. At the other end of the line a well-manicured hand lifted the receiver of an elegant red phone.

'Hello?' The voice was female and refined.

'Hackett here.'

'You were successful?'

'Yeh, an' we got a bonus.'

'Go on.' She didn't sound very enthusiastic about the 'bonus'.

'We got the first locket . . .' Hackett went on to explain the previous night's happenings. 'Anyway, this guy's dad turned out to be Gareth Lester. Well off.' There was a tiny gasp from the other end of the line.

'Hackett, you haven't . . .?'

'They're 'ere. We're gonna get fifty thousand. 'Ow d'you like the sound of that?' he demanded proudly and triumphantly.

'Oh, you fool!' There was a positive note of annoyance in the voice.

'What ya mean?' exclaimed Hackett, crestfallen.

'They're such a *risk*!' she sighed. 'Can't you see, you blithering idiot? You'll have to keep them out of sight wherever you go. If anyone sees them or if they escape we're done for and we won't get our hands on those jewels.'

'You think I'm incapable of stopping them escaping?' growled Hackett unpleasantly.

'Yes, I do,' came the equally unpleasant answer. *'Well, I don't.'*

The Tigress sighed angrily. 'All right, Hackett. They are your responsibility,' she snarled bitterly. 'If you ruin us . . .'

'We'll get that ransom and be glad of it.'

'Well, I hope you can handle it.'

'I can handle it,' he growled.

There was a considerable pause and suddenly the Tigress burst out sharply, 'You say you took possession of the locket last night. Well, what have you been doing this morning? Drinking, smoking, playing cards, getting drunk, I'm sure.' (Coker stifled an explosion of laughter). The woman's voice became even sharper and sterner. 'Well, it's *not* good enough. I don't know why I took you and your lot on! I could easily pick up some guys out of the gutter who'd be willing to work *every single minute* for those jewels. You just sit around wasting time. *Get a move on!* You did a fine job leaving that body in the sea, didn't you? Just ready for the police to find.' She was furious now. 'You're falling to pieces, Hackett. I could take on guys *ten* times better than your slovenly bunch, and I will if you don't pull your socks up. You'd better get off mighty soon. Do you understand?'

Hackett was on the brink of explosion. His face was bright crimson, his eyes bulging, saliva drib-

48

bling on to his chin, teeth gnashing together and his mouth twisted into contortions. His knuckles were white as he gripped the receiver in fury. Blood boiling at the insults, he slammed the receiver back on to the phone with an almighty crash. His fiery eyes burnt fear into all the others in the room. There was a tense silence. Suddenly Hackett leapt to his feet and pounded his fist on the wall. A shower of plaster fluttered to the ground. He began to yell, swearing frequently.

'*The NERVE*! She has the nerve to tell me I'm falling to pieces!' He swung his enraged glare upon his mates. 'It's YOU. YOU'RE falling to pieces! Just *look* at you. Slouched around like animals! You're a lot o' good-fer-nothin's!' He stamped round the room waving his fists and pointed an accusing finger at Rumsey, who cringed. 'YOU – you're always sloshed! And Dudgeon – he can't keep his hands off fags for a second. And as for you, Coker, you're yellow –' as Coker opened his mouth to protest '– yes, a downright coward. You wouldn't say boo to a goose! I'm sick o' the lot o' you!'

Totally lacking self-control, Hackett had allowed his voice to reach a high-pitched scream. Rumsey lurched to his feet.

'ME? Sloshed?' he cried savagely, clenching his fists, to the horror of Michelle, who was a gentle girl.

'Yes!' Hackett roared. 'ABSOLUTELY SLOSH-ED!'

Rumsey was pugnacious and anyone could see

a fight was liable to break out, so the more sensible Sanders exchanged glances with Dudgeon and, stepping forward, gently propelled Hackett to the settee.

'OK. Cool it, Hackett,' he said, while Dudgeon managed to sit Rumsey down and keep him quiet by giving him beer. 'Don't bother messing about with that Rumsey. We must get things organised and show the Tigress we're not the dunderheads she makes out we are.'

Hackett was too exhausted from yelling to bother to argue. He began explaining his plans.

'Since the kid's dad won't be back yet, we'll write a note for 'im to be going on with when 'e gets back. It'll be safe enough if we post it just before we leave 'ere. Then, when 'e's got home, we'll phone with more details. The boy c'n speak to prove 'e's alive.'

'Seems OK,' agreed Hackett. 'An there's no time like the present. Let's do the note.'

Hackett sat down at the table. 'Where're my gloves?' he demanded. 'And a pen and paper.'

Several coats and jackets hung near the door. Dudgeon delved into the pockets of Hackett's grey macintosh and tugged out a pair of smart leather gloves. From his own jacket he produced a black Biro. He tossed the articles on to the table. Hackett slipped on the gloves.

'Paper!'

'Haven't got any,' Dudgeon said. 'Coker'll need to go out an' buy some.' Coker was a stupid-looking man, and he looked even stupider when he let his lower jaw drop several centimetres.

'What! Why –?' he began, his eyes widening under a tangled fringe. Hackett sat back with an exasperated sigh.

'Surely we 'aven't got to wait ten hours while this loony totters off to buy paper? Well, get going, Coker, and you'd better make it snappy!'

'B-but I already went out this morning,' moaned Coker, desperately running his fingers through his dishevelled tufts of ginger hair. Laziness was another of his faults and he was determined to wriggle out of this tiresome errand. 'You could –'

'Shurrup!' bawled Hackett, fed up. 'You know this is what we use you for. You've no guts or muscles and you're lucky we keep you on. If you don't stop fussing over a piffling thing like this . . .'

'Wait a minute, wait a minute,' broke in Sanders. Beneath a chair was a disorderly pile of magazines and newspapers. Sanders flicked through them and drew out two pieces of foolscap. 'I knew there was something.'

Hackett took up the pen and wrote in capitals, neatly and laboriously. John and Michelle crossed to the table silently to watch. Hackett chewed the end of the pen thoughtfully and carried on. Eventually he tossed aside the pen and sank back in his chair, with the air of having finished a great masterpiece. Sanders snatched up the paper and the others gathered round to read it. It said:

'Gareth Lester, we have your son, John, and his cousin, Michelle. We want £50,000 for their safe

51

return. See that you get it or it'll be the worse for the kids. Leave the police out of this or the kids are done for, and wait till we contact you later. The kids'll be OK so long as you keep mum, get the money and wait for further instructions.'

Dudgeon leered. 'Sounds good.'

'Can't say I noticed myself,' muttered John. Luckily he was either ignored or not heard by the men, but Michelle nudged him as if to say anxiously, 'Don't go too far.'

'OK.' Hackett looked up at the cousins. Sign your names. You c'n put a few lines to convince 'im you're still OK.'

John took up the pen and wrote, 'Don't worry, Dad. We'll be fine. John.' Michelle began, 'Dear Uncle Gareth, please tell my parents to try not to worry. I am sure God will help us. You mustn't go around all day sick with worrying. That would only make it worse for us because –' As she wrote Hackett jolted her elbow.

'You don't need to write a book!' he snapped. 'Just sign it!'

Hastily, Michelle finished the sentence with 'we hate to think of you worrying' and signed.

Sanders produced an ink-stained envelope. 'You'd better address it,' he ordered John. The boy could see no point in writing a false address, which would only keep his parents in even worse suspense.

The children were sent to the settee and given magazines to keep them occupied while the men took out road maps, laboriously examined them, and made plans and preparations. As the afternoon dragged by the cousins wondered what was going on. The magazines were boring, full of women with huge smiles, glittering teeth, layers of lipstick, long legs and high-heeled shoes.

The men were obviously preparing for a journey. Sanders and Coker packed the little food from the fridge, while Hackett put maps, papers and torches into a bag. The cousins stiffened when Rumsey brought out Evans's rucksack from behind some chairs.

'We'll dump that on the way,' decided Sanders.

About five o'clock the men drank the last cans of beer from the fridge.

'Let's get going,' suggested Hackett, now in a better mood.

Sanders shrugged. 'Nothing's stopping us. I don't suppose it'll matter if we travel by daylight or dark.'

'Yeh! The sooner we get this boring journey over the better,' Rumsey observed, flinging Dudgeon his anorak. 'It's going to be a terrible squash in the car what with those stupid kids.'

Coker agreed. 'I can't stand cramped journeys. Dudgeon had better sit in the front with Hackett. They're the biggest. You kids will have to squash up. One of you can crouch behind the front seats.'

The men gathered up the few bags and bundles they had. Dudgeon flicked off the light as they stepped into a short empty corridor with stairs leading down to an exit. Sanders locked up the gang's hideout. It was good to be out of the stuffy, smoky room. The refreshing warm air licked the cousins' cheeks as they stepped into a dirty backstreet, pushed along between Rumsey and Dudgeon. There was nothing much to see. There was no pavement, just a narrow road covered in chips of stone and granite. On one side of the road rose a high brick wall, kicked and scratched, on the other side the towering grey building they had just left. It had few windows, some of which were boarded up. The walls were scribbled over and chipped at. The only clean object in sight was a silver Mercedes-Benz parked in front of the doorway they had just passed through. Hackett opened the boot and, after slinging in their baggage, slammed it shut again with a resounding crash. John considered making a break for it but Dudgeon was at his left shoulder and he didn't think it was worth the risk.

Rumsey, Coker and Sanders squashed into the back of the car. John insisted on squatting on the floor so that Michelle could sit on the back seat. Hackett drove and Dudgeon, sitting in the front passenger-seat, opened a packet of cigarettes. Hackett was not a tidy man, but he grew furious if anyone littered his precious car with papers or dropped sticky stuff on the seats. His spotless Mercedes was the apple of his eye. The car engine began to purr and shot off down the backstreet. Hackett turned into a main road. The area was completely unfamiliar to the cousins. They gazed, trying to recognise something and hence calculate where they were. The traffic was busy as people were returning from work. The silver Mercedes stopped at endless red lights and queues of vehicles.

'It'll be all right when we get on to the dual carriageway,' Hackett said; he hated driving slowly. 'Dudgeon! How many times do I have to tell you, if you *must* smoke, *open the window?*'

Dudgeon grunted. Soon the curls of grey smoke were swimming out into the streets amongst the dust from the road, exhaust fumes, noise of burring engines and hoots from car horns. 'Where are we going?' asked John. The men were silent. John repeated the question.

'Never you mind,' muttered Sanders.

'Yes, I *do* mind,' persisted John. 'Wherever it is, I'm going there, so I've a right to know.'

'We've had enough of you for one day,' bawled Hackett. 'Keep quiet.'

But John hadn't finished. He peeped over the driver's seat at the back of Hackett's grizzled head. 'Well, if you won't tell me anything, I'll tell you something. I've said it before, and I'll say it again, my dad can't afford that ransom.'

'Oh, shurrup,' bellowed Hackett, utterly sick of John. 'We've not even sent the note yet, so hold your tongue.'

John kept quiet for a minute, then muttered, 'We can watch the road signs to see where we're going anyway.'

'If you really want to know,' snapped Hackett, 'I don't care a damn if you find out where we're going. You can't do anything about it and we'll not be there long anyway.'

Michelle noticed that the men weren't being very

careful about stopping the cousins from being seen. After all, surely they would be in the papers. Still, John was hidden crouching behind the seat and it would be difficult to see Michelle herself through the window past Sanders's big head.

The car raced on past rows of houses, over bridges and through a town, where it stopped briefly by a red postbox and Hackett hopped out and posted the ransom note. The sky was a misty blue patched with wisps of clouds. The golden sun was low in the sky and shadows grew long. Coker rustled the pages of the *Daily Express* as he struggled desperately with the crossword. Pensively he chewed the end of his pen and, every quarter of an hour, triumphantly filled in a clue.

The swarm of traffic gradually petered out to a few cars and lorries and there were more fields and rivers and less houses in the landscape. From the road signs the cousins discovered that they were travelling north. To pass time Michelle stared at each of the men in turn, wondering how she would describe them to the police if she and John escaped. She started with Rumsey. He was a tall, lanky youth but with strong muscles in his arms. With his sandy hair and whiskers and boyish face some people might have found him handsome, but his bleary eyes betrayed the fact that he drank far more alcohol than was good for him nearly every day of his life. Coker's face always seemed to wear an expression of utter ignorance and bewilderment. His pale grey eyes often displayed fear, especially when Hackett was in a bad temper. He was slim with stout legs and had strands of frizzy ginger hair hanging over his eyes and down the back of his neck. Sanders was well built with a tough but pleasant-looking face, sparkling brown eyes and a mop of brushed dark hair. Dudgeon was broad-shouldered and the biggest of the men. His face was of a dark complexion and often wore a scowl. His greasy hair badly needed cutting. Hackett Michelle could describe without looking at him. She could never forget the square-jawed face and the evil slit-shaped eyes.

After what seemed like hours of driving, the car reached a peaceful village and Hackett drew up beside a public house.

'Fancy a drink?' he asked. It seemed as if Hackett fancied himself as Stirling Moss, because he had been driving his car extremely fast. This appeared to have cheered him up.

'OK,' said Sanders, 'but one of us will 'ave to stay in 'ere to look after these kids.' The men's eyes turned to Coker who was engrossed in the crossword.

'Right, Coker, you stay here with the kids,' confirmed Hackett. 'We'll lock the doors.'

As usual Coker began to protest, but Sanders broke in, 'We'll bring you a can out here –'

'Why do I have be lumbered with two –?'

'Look, do your crossword.'

Coker slouched back in his seat sulkily. The car doors slammed shut and Hackett, Sanders, Dudgeon and Rumsey strolled into the public house for some beer. John got up on to the back seat beside

Coker and Michelle. He craned his neck to look at the crossword. Coker had marked in a few words in an untidy hand. He was wrestling with the other clues.

'Dionysus,' said John.

'What?' Coker looked up, bewildered.

'Six across – Dionysus – he's the Greek god of wine. D-I-O-N-Y-S-U-S.'

'Oh,' said Coker and filled it in. Michelle couldn't stop herself from admiring John as he leant over Coker, pointing out the answers to the clues much to Coker's embarrassment. She found him very handsome, and she felt proud that he was her cousin.

'Finished it yet, John?' she asked. He flashed her a grin.

'Not quite.'

Michelle fell to thinking about her parents and Mrs Hodge. What was happening to her and John didn't seem real. She knew it was, but it didn't *seem* real.

She glanced at the car door to her left. She only had to lift the lock and leap out . . . If Coker yelled to his mates, she could call for help from the villagers. The men had been in the pub for ages. She lifted the lock – it clicked. Coker looked up.

'Hey –' he began. She swung the door open and put one foot on the pavement – but, at that moment, Sanders, Hackett, Rumsey and Dudgeon came jostling out of the pub. Sanders, the most sober, started and took a hurried step forward. Michelle realised it was too late. She lifted her foot back into the car. Sanders climbed in angrily.

'Coker, what were you playing at?' Without waiting for a reply he turned to Michelle. 'You wouldn't have got away anyway. I gave Coker my gun before we left.'

'Your gun?' She had never really believed that they had guns, as she hadn't seen them.

'My gun. Give me it back, Coker.' A gleaming black revolver was passed in front of the cousins to Sanders. 'Hackett's got one too, so don't try anything funny, kids.'

This time Michelle insisted on crouching behind the driver's seat. The other men clambered into the car, unusually merry. Rumsey swayed about singing. Even Hackett had a drunken grin on his face. Dudgeon muttered a joke and the other men chuckled. Michelle was slightly frightened. Hackett was driving and he wasn't one hundred per cent sober. It could be dangerous. However, Hackett, though still racing along, seemed to be all right.

'What about that can o' beer you said you'd get me?' demanded Coker.

'Sorry, ole chap. Forgot,' grinned Dudgeon, displaying an uneven row of yellow teeth.

'Well, I don't much care,' grunted Coker. 'I don't want to get drunk like you lot.'

'Drunk?' grinned Rumsey.

'Yes, drunk.'

'*I'm* not drunk,' exclaimed Sanders indignantly and truthfully. 'It's those three.'

The cousins were amazed when Hackett replied cheerfully, 'Come on – a bit o' drink does us good.

Why shouldn't we enjoy ourselves?' The drink had put him in good spirits.

As the long, monotonous journey continued and the light became dimmer, Michelle, crouching behind the driver's seat, said a silent prayer. John looked serious; he was worrying although he tried not to. He couldn't stop thinking about his parents and home. It was cramped and stuffy in the car. The air smelt and tasted of Dudgeon's foul tobacco. The Mercedes sped on to another stretch of dual carriageway and Hackett drove even faster, making their heads spin. He began to hum drunkenly and his driving was reckless. He overtook lorries dangerously and ignored the objections of his passengers. A short way ahead were some road-works, and a set of traffic lights had been set up there. The lights were changing from green to red and Hackett was determined to get past before the red light lit up. He accelerated. But the lorry in front had a more sensible driver and stopped at the traffic lights instead of zooming past. Hackett's Mercedes came tearing along behind the lorry.

'LOOK OUT!' yelled John, seeing the lorry stop. Hackett pulled on the brakes, clenching his teeth. The wild screeching of the car rent the air, but the Mercedes refused to come to a halt. The passengers in the car caught their breath, eyes widening in terror. The nose of the Mercedes crashed into the back of the lorry with a deafening clatter, screech of brakes and hiss of steam.

chapter four

Flight In The Forest

The impact of the crash threw them all forward in their seats, and, if the brakes had not slowed down the car as much as they had, both Hackett and Dudgeon would have been flung through the front window. The grating of metal set their teeth on edge and the windscreen shattered, the tiny slivers of glass giving a frosty effect. Their breath came out in shaky gasps; their hearts leapt about in terror. Steam from the radiator spat upwards, hissing viciously, and condensed on the windows.

'Get out!' Hackett's voice was hoarse with shock. 'Make a break for those trees – and don't let the kids be seen.' Breathing rather unevenly, Sanders whipped out his gun.

'You'll run for those trees or else get a bullet in your back,' he said sharply. Rumsey forced open a door and coils of steam swam into the car. As they were pushed out on to the road, the cousins were aware of Sanders behind them with the gun. When they hesitated, he snarled menacingly, 'I mean it.'

Other cars were skidding to a halt; people leapt out and rushed to the scene. The cousins were bustled to the roadside. Reluctantly, they hurried up a slope into a cluster of tall pine trees. Hackett

paused to grab a bag and the incriminating rucksack out of the car boot. Shouting broke out as
people crowded round the crushed Mercedes, and
the approaching mob sent Hackett tearing away
towards the pines. He found his mates and the
cousins crouching behind trees. Dudgeon was panting heavily and whimpering after the running.

'Get moving!' gasped Hackett. 'We'll be followed. Cops'll be here any minute.'

There was no time for the gang to rebuke Hackett
for causing the accident. They scrambled to their
feet and wound their way in and out of the pines.
Hackett was lugging along the baggage. He threw
the rucksack at Coker.

'Carry something, you lout.'

As they scrambled on, the wail of a police siren
was audible in the distance.

'Wait – please – wait,' gasped Dudgeon, who was
struggling behind, too exhausted to run.

'Aw, shurrup! Move!' yelled Hackett. They
reached the other side of the pine wood and found
themselves in fields which sloped upwards to a
forest denser than the pine wood.

'We'll head for there,' Hackett said. Sanders
rounded on him.

'Hackett, you've blown us!' He pointed through
the trees to where two policemen were talking to a
lorry-driver who was indicating the pine wood. Also
visible through the trees was the car wreck surrounded by crowds and policemen.

'Well, get a move on to that forest,' growled
Hackett. The sun was rapidly sinking. Their legs

ached as they hurried towards the forest. John deliberately moved without speed, trying to slow the men down; but they could see he wasn't going as fast as he could. Sanders caught him by the arm and tugged him along.

'Look, remember the guns,' he panted. 'If you're holding us up we might have to get rid of you.' It was too dangerous to try to yell. Besides, the cousins hadn't the breath: and they were too far away for the police to hear.

The sinking sun sent their shadows stretching across the field. Sweat broke out on their foreheads; their backs were hunched and heads drooping. They reached a fence and tumbled over it. The field they were crossing now was crusted with mud which had been baked hard and then had cracked in the hot sun. As they reached the shade of the forest, Dudgeon was still struggling over the fence. Far away, in the pine wood, they could see figures moving about. They worked their way into the heart of the forest and leant against trees or sank to the ground. The gnarled trunks stretched to great heights, splitting into branches and blossoming to form a leafy green roof. The forest floor was matted with pine needles, and green plants sprang from it, clustering round the tree roots. A few golden rays of sunlight, which had squeezed through the barrage of whispering leaves, crisscrossed in the air, lighting up floating particles of dust and forming flickering shadows at the feet of the weary men and the cousins. The atmosphere was hot and stuffy as if a storm was brewing. The breeze was too gentle to knock over a straw standing on its end. As Coker flung the rucksack he had been carrying on to the mat of pine needles, John sat down with his back to a tree, wiping the sweat from his brow. He wished desperately that he had risked yelling for help as soon as they had climbed out of the car wreck. Surely the men wouldn't have dared to shoot the cousins in broad daylight in front of crowds of people . . . or would they? Michelle squatted on her heels, tossing a stone from hand to hand, wondering if there was any way they could have escaped. Rumsey opened his shirt, while Coker fanned himself with the newspaper he had kept in his pocket. Hackett stood with one hand resting on a tree trunk, peering through a tangle of branches and twigs. He was watching Dudgeon still scrabbling over the stony field, his back bent so that his hands nearly touched the ground. Perspiration discoloured his shirt and ran over his face.

'What does Dudgeon think he's playing at?' snapped Hackett. 'Some cop's bound to see him.'

'It's OK. He's keeping in the shadows.' Sanders stepped to Hackett's side, deciding it was time the man took the scolding he well deserved. Sanders's eyes were fiery. 'You can't complain, Hackett! It was you who got us into this mess! Driving along as if you owned the world. Well, the Tigress isn't going to be too pleased when she hears about it!' For once Hackett was silent. Dudgeon had reached the outskirts of the forest. He staggered towards them and dropped to his knees by a huge oak.

'That's what you get for all that smoking,'

grinned Sanders. 'It's a laugh to see a big strong bloke like you staggering along. It's the fags that do it.' Dudgeon just continued to pant incessantly. Michelle felt slightly sorry for him.

'D'you think we've shook off the cops?' Rumsey asked.

'There's no sign of them,' Sanders said. 'It makes me sick to think we could still be driving with not too far to go. You, Hackett –' with utter loathing ' – Gah!'

'Oh, shurrup. It was Rumsey that kept on buying more 'n' more drinks.'

'Oh, so you admit you'd had too much?' Hackett's face clouded over.

'Look, I'm just sick at losing that car. You know how I loved it. I've been pretty patient. I 'aven't blown my top yet. So you'd better stop rubbing it in. You're not going to do any good going on like this.'

'Well,' boomed Sanders, 'what're you going to do now? You've blown us. What do you suggest now?'

'Yeh.' Rumsey rose to his feet, fists clenched. 'What're you gonna do now?'

Hackett snarled.

'Nick another motor; what d'you think?'

'Oh, yeh,' bawled Rumsey with heavy sarcasm. ' "Nick another motor," he says, as calm as that. You nut! *Where from?*'

' 'Ave you no brains at all, Rumsey?' demanded Hackett. 'We'll nick one from a farm or somethin'.'

'Oh, yeh,' began Rumsey. 'An' where – ?'

'Aw shurrup,' bawled Hackett. 'Now listen, if you want ter get anywhere. We'll make our way along till we come ter a farm or something and nick a truck. We . . .'

Hackett droned on, trying to convince his mates, and examining a map. Michelle and John exchanged glances, which said 'Shall we make a break for it?' They edged away from the men. If they did run they would have to be speedy before the men got their guns out. They doubted whether the gang would shoot; someone might hear the blast.

Then came a stroke of luck as far as they were concerned. Lightning flashed, making the trees stand out in clear-cut silhouettes for less than a second. Coker stiffened; his eyes widened.

'Lightning,' he whispered.

'So what?' boomed Hackett. 'We'll stay here a bit until the commotion on the road has died down. It'll be dimmer soon and we can go and nick a motor.'

'But – but – ' stammered Coker.

'But what?'

'That was lightning. We'd better get out of this forest.'

'What on earth for?'

As he spoke, Michelle and John were edging farther away from the men, unnoticed.

'Why, if we stay here we're more likely to be killed,' stammered Coker. 'There are so many trees and if just *one* was struck it could either fall on us or set the whole forest on fire and we'd be trapped . . .'

'Oh, don't be yellow,' snapped Hackett, disgusted at Coker's behaviour, but Coker was convinced that he was right, and he was genuinely scared.

The lightning flashed again and shortly afterwards the grumbling clouds emitted a roll of thunder, though without any rain. Coker shivered.

'Look! One of us could be dead by now.'

'Don't be a nut, Coker,' Sanders said. 'It's miles away, anyhow.'

Coker's eyes were wide with fear, as he glanced desperately at his companions.

'Look, are you all crazy? Haven't you heard about people getting struck down, especially where there are trees which could – '

'You dunderhead!' Rumsey broke in. 'It's a chance in a million.'

'Well, if you're going to stay here to be killed, I'm not!' blustered Coker. He began to run.

The men moved after him. Michelle glanced at John, who nodded. They tore off in the opposite direction, dodging behind trees. Hackett turned as he heard their pounding footsteps. He swore out loud in agitation and whipped his gun from his pocket. He didn't want to hurt the cousins, only to frighten them. Rumsey took up the chase with Hackett while the others dashed after Coker. John, his fair hair falling into his eyes, decided to head back to the road. He was a fast runner, second fastest in his class at school. He swallowed and his heart jumped as Hackett fired. The bullet crunched into the dry wood of a stout tree trunk. John charged through a bush; the twigs scratched his arms, and brushed against his cheek. He did not know where Michelle, Hackett and Rumsey had gone. But as he reached the edge of the forest, where the number of trees and firs with green-fringed branches petered out, he saw Hackett and Rumsey in the fields looking towards him. They had expected him to come this way. John turned, eyes bright with determination, and dodged back among the trees, hotly pursued. He didn't care where he went now as long as he got away. As he hurried through the forest, twittering birds crossed his path and rustled the leaves above him, and a delightful baby rabbit bounded out of some bushes; but John did not notice them. He was intent on losing the men. He reached the other side of the forest and, seeing no sign of the gang, crouched in some long grass to rest and recover his breath. Before him stretched a grassy and rock-covered valley, and beyond that, tiny in the far distance, was a group of houses. Freedom, John thought, if he could get there. He heard voices in the forest and scrambled to his feet. This time there were no trees to cover him. His feet pounded on the grass. Then, to his dismay, he heard a triumphant cry and other footsteps besides his own. John, set with determination, tore on, breathing heavily. He came to a steep slope covered in loose rocks and rubble. He had to work his way down cautiously. But suddenly his foot slipped on a wobbling rock! With a horrified gasp he tumbled backwards, his elbow hitting the stones, and sharp bits of rock sticking into his back.

'Stop!' commanded a harsh voice. He threw a

despairing glance over his shoulder. At the top of the slope stood Hackett, legs apart, gun pointed straight at John. The boy scrambled painfully to his feet and climbed up over the rubble. As he neared the top of the slope Hackett caught his arm and pulled him the rest of the way up. John brushed the dust and flakes of stone from his clothing. He scowled at a fierce-looking Hackett.

'Caught Michelle yet?' John asked, coolly.

Hackett didn't answer. John took this to mean 'no' and smiled to himself.

Michelle had run out of a different part of the forest. The wind had played with her long chestnut locks and tangled them. Sweat was sticking the back of her blouse to her back. To add to the discomfort, the heat and stuffiness in the atmosphere had not vanished. Michelle's aching feet trampled down the grass. When she came out of the forest she did not yet feel safe. She had heard the shot from Hackett's gun . . . She was struck with fear for John. But surely there would have been a yell if he had been shot? Maybe not. But Michelle decided she should not go back to appease the fears of her imagination. Her ears detected the sound of running water. Yes; as she ran on she came to a gurgling river glistening in the setting sun. The water looked red where sunlight hit it. Even in the present circumstances, Michelle could not help admiring the beauty of the sunset. The sky looked as if a paintbrush had been drawn across it, leaving pink streaks mingled with violet. Purple clouds gathered on the horizon, fringed with gold from the sun. The sun itself was a fiery red, circled with yellow and orange.

Michelle decided to swim across the river: it would be a barrier between her and the crooks. Then she heard the men shouting in the forest. Panic seized her and she began to hurry. She tugged off her flat sandals and tucked the hem of her skirt into her belt so it would not hinder her during swimming. She slipped herself over the bank, which was a mass of overhanging earth and tangled roots. The cold water swirled round her legs. In she went with a mighty shiver. Frothy ripples gushed round her shoulders and surged into her face. The current tumbled her hair around in the water. With goose-pimples covering her arms, she broke into a front crawl and bravely struggled to defeat the fast-flowing current. The muddy river bed plunged to great depths. Her arms pounded the water, splashing her hot face and washing away the sweat. She coughed and choked as a gush of water and silt surged into her mouth. At last, gasping for breath, she reached the other bank. Her hand grabbed at a tuft of long grass and she began to scramble out, soaked to the skin. Suddenly she froze as a menacing voice from the bank behind her cried,

'Stop and swim back or your cousin's dead!'

With wide eyes she turned her head. On the other side of the river stood Hackett, Sanders, Rumsey, Dudgeon, Coker and John. Hackett was pointing his gun as John's head.

chapter five

Danger In The Dark

Wearily, Michelle slipped back into the chilly water. Her progress was slow as she struck out for the opposite bank. She glanced at the grim faces of the men and at John. Her cousin looked furious with himself. His fair head was hung. He knew that Michelle might have escaped if he had not been caught. They had both been so near freedom! Coker had been calmed by Dudgeon and Sanders. He was quiet and looked scared. There had been no more lightning. The cousins never knew what had happened amongst Sanders, Dudgeon and Coker, but somehow sense had been knocked into Coker. Michelle clambered on to the bank and, panting, put on her sandals. John bit his lip as he watched her shivering, with water running down her and dampening the ground. She was beginning to wonder if she had acted rashly to jump into the river. Where was she going to get a change of clothes? The men didn't seem to care about her being drenched. Hackett wafted his gun about.

'Remember I have this all the time,' he said. 'You might think you were smart running away, but I could easily have shot you as you ran if I'd wanted. But I reckoned we'd catch you and I want that ransom. However, if you're causing us bother we might decide we'd be better off without you.' He gesticulated with the revolver. '*Don't try it again*,' he added fiercely. He nodded at Michelle. 'And if you catch pneumonia, I won't be sorry.'

'But aren't you going to *do* anything?' demanded John, staring wide-eyed at the glowering Hackett.

'What d'you mean, do anythin'?' growled the man.

'Well, she can't go around in those soaking clothes – '

'*Wot*? She jolly well can – and will! You don't think I'm gonna provide her with clothes if she decides to jump in a river like a loony?'

John was silent. He strode on with a sullen face, thinking black thoughts.

The light had grown dim. It was as if a grey veil had been hung before their eyes. The men seemed to know where they were going as they led the children over the grass, which bristled with violet thistles. Shadows stole across the land, stealthily, surreptitiously, and crept over the path of crushed grass the crooks took, so that the place was a dim scene of grey and blue patches, their continuity broken by the faint silhouettes of twisting trees, whose branches clawed the twilight with their evil twig fingers. Coker shivered when another fork of lightning cracked the sky. Billowing grey clouds gathered above, whispering and conspiring, and the air seemed even stuffier. Michelle shivered in her damp clothes as she walked briskly to match the men's huge strides.

'I think that's a farmhouse,' Hackett said, pointing to the unclear outline of a building not far off. As they strode on they came to a stone dyke surrounding a field. They scrambled over the wall and made their way across the field towards the building. A sheep trotted over and stared at them suspiciously. Then it gave a disapproving bleat and hurried off to its mates. John yawned and rubbed his eyes. He and Michelle were both feeling the strain of the long journey and their desperate escape attempts. They reckoned it could be any time between ten and eleven o'clock. There was only a trickle of moonlight squeezing out from between clouds. At last they reached the building and the children discovered it *was* a farmhouse. Nearby stood a pigsty and a barn. A disturbed hen's cackling was faintly audible and the smell of pigs reached their nostrils. The concrete area round the farmhouse was patched with mud and strewn with strands of hay and hens' meal. There was no sign of any farmworkers and only one light showed at the front of the house. The men and cousins worked their way to the back of the building which cast a gloomy shadow over a yard. The men spoke in low whispers. In the yard was a small dark-coloured farm lorry.

'This is pretty handy,' observed Dudgeon.

'Yeh,' agreed Hackett. 'If the kids are in the back, they'll be out of sight.'

'OK. Let's get it out of here,' murmured Sanders 'Hackett, you're not driving!'

'Shurrup! We'll decide who's driving when we

73

get the lorry on to the road.' He tried the driver's door. 'Locked. Get started on it, Sanders.'

'The back isn't locked,' Coker discovered.

'Good. Dump the bags in there and keep the noise down.'

Sanders fished out a piece of wire and quickly succeeded in picking the lock. Hackett scrambled up and released the brake. The other men gathered behind the lorry and began to push it out of the yard, forcing the cousins to help them and threatening them not to make a noise. Hackett turned the steering-wheel to direct the vehicle into the lane which ran from the farmhouse through the fields. With all the men pushing, the lorry did not seem too heavy. The only sound was the crunch of the tyres on the gravel, and heavy breathing. The lane came out at a narrow road, where Sanders climbed into the front beside Hackett. The other men clambered into the back with the cousins. The only things in it were a few wooden boxes containing hens' feathers and straw, in which the farmer had probably taken his hens to market.

The engine started and the lorry began to move: Sanders must have used his piece of wire instead of an ignition key.

In the back of the lorry it was pitch dark. Dudgeon and Rumsey had torches, but they didn't want to waste the batteries. Still wet through, Michelle shivered. It was uncomfortable sitting in a puddle of water. Dudgeon struck a match. As he lifted it to light a cigarette, the golden flame made flickering patterns on his face. When he put out the match only the red glow of the cigarette-end signified his presence. The smoke was stifling. Coker began to cough.

'Put that thing out!' he snapped, seeming tense and anxious, but Dudgeon was enjoying his smoke and continued.

Hackett drove on for a while, then abruptly pulled into a parking place at the roadside sheltered by drooping bushes.

'What've we stopped for?' Rumsey asked alarmed, as Dudgeon's eyes darted about worriedly and Coker stiffened.

'Dunno.' Dudgeon opened up the back of the lorry and climbed out followed by Coker, while Rumsey knelt on the floor and peered outside. They heard the cab door slam as Sanders stepped out.

'What's up?' the cousins heard Dudgeon call. They could imagine Sanders's grim countenance as he explained.

'Hackett saw a copper's car further up the road. We've stopped till it has time to disappear. Cops'll probably be looking out for this lorry by now, especially after the accident.' At this a gleam of hope flickered in the cousins' eyes and Rumsey, still in the lorry peering out, grunted discontentedly.

'Well, make sure you give it time to get clear,' Dudgeon advised.

'You think we haven't thought of that?' snarled Sanders scornfully.

At that moment the storm broke. The rain hammered furiously on the roof of the lorry. The incessant pounding was deafening. Rumsey hastily shut the door and shrank back with a wet fringe and a blob of rain on his nose. In a few moments the door was slid open again and Dudgeon and Coker clambered back into the lorry, their clothes glistening with rain. While the lorry door was open, the rain was even louder and fell in hair-thin pillars before the cousins' eyes, forming a watery screen. Shivering, Coker vigorously slammed the door shut and Rumsey flicked on a torch. The shaft of dusty light intruded into the inky blackness and threw bulky shadows over the sides of the lorry. The air smelt of damp clothes. After a time the vehicle jolted into movement, and splashed through puddles. Sanders had now taken over the driving from Hackett. Rumsey did not leave the torch on for very long and presently began to snore.

Despite her wet clothes and the hard floor of the lorry, Michelle soon fell asleep, followed by John. The storm continued to rage; Sanders continued to drive. He drove all through the night, peering through the nearly opaque sheet of rain. Fields and hills stretched from either side of the road. Mountains rose in the distance.

John reluctantly opened his eyes. Someone was shaking him awake – Dudgeon. It took a couple of seconds for John to realise he was still in the back of the lorry. As before, the rain was pounding on the roof, but not so heavily; it was more of a gentle patter. The door at the back of the lorry was open. Rumsey and Michelle were climbing out. The light was pale grey. It might have been three or four o'clock in the morning. John yawned rudely in Dudgeon's face. He wearily sat up rubbing his eyes.

'Now, keep quiet and don't bother us,' snapped Dudgeon, as John climbed out of the lorry. He stared round in amazement as he stretched his limbs.

'Where's this?' he asked curiously.

'Never you mind!' was the gruff reply as Dudgeon slammed shut the door.

Before John stood a huge mansion-type house. It was built of grey stone. Ivy and other leafy plants crept up the walls and clung round the windows. It was indeed very attractive. The stone walls were rainwashed and the window panes splattered with glistening drops of rain. Wide steps led up to the doorway. There were no other buildings in sight. Trees, grass and woody areas surrounded the house. It was an old building and needed some repairs. It looked very deserted and unlived in.

Coker suddenly came running from behind the house and called, 'Hey! There *is* a place to hide the lorry. A shed.'

'Great.' Hackett nodded to Rumsey. 'You drive round while we find Cox.' Rumsey scrambled into the cab and steered the vehicle round the back of the house. Hackett, Sanders and Coker strode on towards the front door.

'Go on!' Dudgeon said to the cousins, nodding towards his mates.

Michelle joined John as they walked along the

77

grassy track leading to the steps. Rain spat in their faces and dropped through the trees. Michelle spoke to John in a low voice.

'While you were asleep the men called this Cox's place and talked about getting his locket. What d'you think they want lockets for?'

'I've no idea. It's a mystery to me,' replied John.

The cousins stood on the bottom step as Hackett thundered on the door with his fist, his hair shining with rain. There was no sound from within the house.

John whispered to Michelle. 'Do you know whereabouts this place is?'

Michelle pointed beyond the treetops where mountains rose majestically, their peaks hidden by misty clouds.

'The scenery looks like the Highlands. We must have come a long way north.'

'Shurrup!' growled Hackett, who had heard her mumbling to John. He continued hammering on the door. Someone stirred in the house. As the rain poured down, Michelle shuddered in her damp clothes. The huge front door swung inwards. In the doorway stood a sleepy-eyed little woman, wrapped in a checked dressing-gown, with her grey hair piled in a net, and wearing some red slippers far too big for her.

'What kind of a time is this tae come knocking at the door? Some folks have nae – ' She stopped short as she caught sight of the gun Hackett had whipped out. The woman shrank back like a timid mouse.

'Finley Cox,' Hackett said. 'Where is Finley Cox?'

The poor woman's mouth opened and shut like a goldfish's.

'He's – he's in – in his bed,' she stammered.

Hackett barged into the hall, closely followed by Coker and Sanders. Reluctantly John and Michelle entered, with Dudgeon behind them. Rumsey came running up and stomped in after them, panting. The little woman stared at the cousins with wide watery eyes. Hackett glanced briefly round the hall at the dusty pictures on the wall and faded wallpaper. His fierce gaze fell on the terrified old woman.

'You'll be the owner who rents this place to Cox?' suggested Hackett. Her bony hands shaking, she gulped and shook her head.

'Well, *who are you, then?*' boomed Hackett. The frail creature trembled all over.

'M-Miss McNab, the – the housekeeper.'

'Well, take us to Cox's room.' Miss McNab did not hesitate. She scurried up the stairs, clutching the banister. She led them along the landing to a wooden panelled door, knocked gently on it and hurried in. The men stomped into the room with the cousins. Dudgeon closed the door and positioned himself in front of it with Rumsey. In a huge bed a plump man with a tufty brown beard was asleep. At the foot of the bed lay a huge hound. As the men entered his master's room, the dog lifted its head and pricked up its ears. It began to yelp incessantly and leapt at Hackett, saliva glistening round its white teeth, fur bristling on its neck and pink tongue lolling out of its mouth. Its forepaws were on Hackett's chest and its head level with the man's face. It looked as if at any moment it would bite a chunk out of Hackett. Forced to look at the hound's fierce eyes and gnashing teeth, Hackett for once seemed scared. The man in the bed, woken by the baying, was rubbing his eyes and taking in the scene with amazement. The other members of the gang stood as if paralysed.

'Call this dog off or I'll shoot it,' growled Hackett, managing to keep his voice steady.

'But what – ?' began the man in the bed, sitting up and displaying red and blue striped pyjamas.

'I said – call this dog off or I'll *shoot it*!' Hackett yelled, his voice almost drowned by the hound's baying. 'Call it off, Cox!'

The utterly dazed Cox rubbed his beard and shouted, 'Wagner. Sit! *Sit*, Wagner! Quiet, boy . . .' Eventually the dog slouched down at the foot of the bed, breathing heavily through flared nostrils, its chest sinking and rising, its muzzle soaked in saliva. It bared its teeth and stared savagely at Hackett. There was a tense hush in the room. Cox stared at Hackett from under bristly brown eyebrows. Hackett approached the bed with his gun erect.

'Who the blazes are you?' demanded Cox. Hackett smirked.

'Just someone very interested in lockets.' At the word 'lockets' Cox started.

'What do *you* know about – ?' He broke off.

'Oh, quite a lot,' Hackett said, anticipating the rest of the question. 'That's why we came here. We'd like your silver locket. I'm afraid you won't be getting any of the jewels.' Finley Cox pursed his lips and a furious look crossed his countenance.

'You can't have it. You don't think we're going to let *you* get our jewels? Webb will deal with you.' Hackett gave a mock laugh.

'But, of course, how could you know that we're working with Webb's sister – the Tigress?'

'So *that*'s how you know!'

'Yes, Cox. And every move Webb makes is traced by his sister. You may as well forget about having those jewels now. We've already disposed of Evans – ' an expression of amazement and fright grew on Cox's face ' – alias Sewell,' added Hackett smugly. The cousins glanced quickly at each other. So their suspicions about Evans's identity had been correct.

Cox was trying to hide his fear as he flung aside his sheet and swung his feet on to the floor. It all seemed too much for him. He ran his fingers through the little hair he had. The top of his head was pink and bald. He tried to avoid catching sight of Hackett's revolver as he reached for a tartan dressing-gown.

'What happens if I give you the locket?' asked Cox.

'Then we'd like to stay here for a bit. Bin driving all night, see?'

'I meant what happens *to me* if I give you the locket?' Cox snapped impatiently, tying the cord of his dressing-gown.

'Oh, you'll be all right. Let's have it.'

With a reluctant sigh Cox strode to a painting of some fruit which hung on the wall. Behind it was a tiny safe. Cox opened it.

'Aha! Very neat!' exclaimed Hackett. 'One of those, is it? What else 'ave you got in there?' He crossed to the safe and drew out a sapphire ring, a jade necklace and a box containing several bank-notes. 'Thank you very much. Very kind of you,' grinned Hackett, slipping the notes and jewellery inside his jacket. 'Stolen, I presume. You *are* a naughty boy, Cox!'

Crimson with rage, Cox opened his mouth to speak, but Hackett wafted the gun near his nose with a warning look and reached out his hand for the locket which Cox had removed from the safe. Cox unfolded his fingers. A silver heart-shaped locket lay in his sticky palm. Hackett took the identical one that had belonged to Evans out of his pocket and looked at them closely.

'OK. That's fine. Now' – to Miss McNab – 'how about some breakfast? It's early, but we're all starving.' Miss McNab nodded hastily and looked very relieved when Hackett returned the gun to the inside of his jacket.

Cox led the way down to the dining-room, where a large rain-splattered window looked out over the grass, trees and heather. A door led off into the adjoining kitchen.

'Go and keep an eye on 'er, Rumsey,' ordered Hackett as the housekeeper bustled through it; Rumsey followed. Dudgeon, Coker and Hackett flung themselves on to a couch. Dudgeon lit a cigarette while Sanders took a newspaper out of a rack and started to read it. Cox just sat staring into thin air and looking glum.

An odour of eggs frying drifted into the room. John and Michelle were positioned on wooden chairs near the window. They wanted to talk but, excluding the rustle of the newspaper, there was a silence in the room and neither of them liked to break it. Outside, the rain had stopped but was still dripping through the trees. The clock on the mantelpiece showed twenty past four. Presently Miss McNab entered, sagging a little under the weight of a tray holding six plates of fried eggs, closely followed by Rumsey, who was carrying three more. While the men and Miss McNab sat round the table, John and Michelle tucked into their breakfasts on the couch.

It was five o'clock when, yawning, the cousins went into the kitchen to help Miss McNab wash up. Finding that the kitchen window was wedged tightly shut, Sanders locked the back door and took the key away before returning to the dining-room, from which the men's voices drifted in. For a moment the idea of smashing the window crossed John's mind, but he realised that the noise would bring the men rushing in before he and Michelle could climb through and escape. Through the window they could see that the storm was over. The rain seemed to have washed and cleaned the sky because it was now a hazy, yet polished, blue merged with the tiniest white wisps of clouds. The early morning sun lit up the tips of leaves in gold and made the puddles twinkle and glisten. In the kitchen, curled up in a wicker basket, was a handsome young tortoiseshell cat. Michelle squatted down to stroke him.

'His name is Sebastian,' Miss McNab said proudly.

'Does he belong to you?'

'Oh, aye. He's nae mair than two years old. Here, young lad, here's a plate fer ye tae dry.' Michelle joined John and they dried the dishes together.

'Do you know anything about these lockets and jewels?' John asked hopefully in a low voice.

'Aye, I do. An' Mr Cox, he had promised tae give me some o' the money he got for the jewels when he an' his mates found them. But I dinnae ken what'll happen noo Mr Cox has lost the locket. He'll nae get his share an' I'll nae get mine. 'Tis nae fair. 'Twas Mr Cox who helped steal the jewels. Why should these good-for-nothings have them?' She gave a little sigh and lifted a pile of yolk-smeared dishes into the washing-up basin.

'So Cox is a thief?' exclaimed Michelle.

'Aye, an' I suppose I'm just as bad, ye ken, bein' in league with him, like.'

'Oh!' Michelle said.

'But where *are* the stolen jewels and what have the lockets got to do with them?' John asked excitedly.

'Ye mean ye dinnae ken?' Miss McNab sounded astonished.

'I wouldn't ask if I knew.' John was getting impatient to solve the mystery.

'Well, I'm nae sure if I should tell ye if ye havenae heard about it already!'

'But why not?' asked John, utterly disappointed.

'Och, I cannae tell ye,' was all Miss McNab could say. John was fed up. He had one more try.

'You can trust us. Do tell us. We're dying to know,' he urged.

'But I dinnae ken who ye are an' what ye are doin' here. How come ye ter be with these men, a young lad and lassie?'

'We're being held to ransom,' explained Michelle.

Miss McNab started. She was about to question them further when an idea struck John and he burst in, 'Is there a telephone in this house?'

'Nay, nay, lad.'

'Pity,' John thought. 'We could have tried phoning the police.'

'What d'ye mean, ye are bein' held to ransom?' asked Miss McNab curiously, her eyes dancing with excitement.

'We'll answer your questions if you tell us about the lockets,' John said firmly. Miss McNab turned away, shaking her head.

'Nay, nay, I dinnae think I should,' she muttered. The cousins returned to the dining-room while Miss McNab put out some cat food for Sebastian's breakfast. The men were slouched around the room, discussing some football news they had found in a newspaper. Cox's brow was creased with

85

worry. John and Michelle sleepily sat down and talked together quietly, trying to solve the mystery of the lockets. All they knew was that Cox and some other people, possibly including Evans, were looking for stolen jewels. Somehow the lockets fitted in and Hackett's gang, led by the Tigress, was trying to get hold of these lockets. The Tigress had a brother called Webb whom she presumably spied on, thus obtaining information for her gang. These facts were some of the pieces of a complicated jig-saw, but the cousins did not yet know how to fit them together.

Dudgeon stubbed out a cigarette and Hackett put down a newspaper. He crossed his legs, placed his fingertips together and smiled wickedly at Cox.

'Now, dear old chap,' began Hackett, 'you've had time to digest your breakfast. I'd like to ask a few questions.' His voice was cheerful and smug. 'How about telling us your plans? What had you arranged? Where were you all going to meet with your lockets?'

'Why should I tell *you*?' snapped Cox.

'Because,' replied Hackett as cheerful as ever, casually bringing out his gun, 'if you don't, I'll shoot you.' Cox's eyes flashed angrily.

'Now, where were you going to meet Grier, Yates and Evans?' prodded Hackett.

Cox thoughtfully twisted a tuft of his beard, obviously wondering whether or not to tell the truth.

'Here,' he growled, unwillingly.

Hackett raised his eyebrows and twirled the revolver between his fingers.

'Just as I reckoned. We knew Evans was comin' 'ere, and I figured it wouldn't be long before Yates and Grier turned up. When exactly will they arrive?'

Cox shrugged. 'Yates was travelling from London to Grier's place and then the two of them were to come up here. It depends how long the journeys take.'

'I see. Well, we'll wait for them here. Hope you don't mind.'

'Can I go and get dressed?' growled Cox.

'No, no, old chap. You might get up to mischief. We couldn't have that, could we? Do you have any cards? We could play poker! Ha! What a brainwave. Well, come on, Cox old bean, get out the cards.'

As the men rose to gather round the table, Sanders passed the window and froze.

'Hackett. Over here!' Hackett strode to his side and Sanders nodded through the window. A skinny boy with dishevelled hair was wheeling a red motorbike through the trees, looking very bedraggled. Hackett called over Cox.

'Who's that?' Hackett's voice had turned menacing.

Cox lifted his shoulders. 'How should I know?'

The boy was now approaching the door of the mansion. The cousins were excited. Perhaps they could signal to the boy, who could have read about them in a newspaper. But the chances of signalling were slim with the men there.

'McNab!' Hackett summoned the nervous old

woman. She appeared in the doorway, fingering the cuffs of her sleeves. Hackett drew out his revolver. 'Answer the door! See what the boy wants but don't let him in. And if you try to tell him we're here or get help, you won't live a second longer.' Hackett had no difficulty in forcing Miss McNab to obey. She apprehensively shuffled to the door. Daylight streamed into the hall as Hackett listened from the dining-room door, out of sight. The boy's perky voice drifted into the room.

'Telegram fer Mr Cox, missus.'

'Thank ye,' stammered Miss McNab. But the freckled-faced young Scot was a loquacious chap.

'It's a lang way up tae git here,' he remarked. 'An' the road's all muddy after the storm. Aye, bad storm, 'twas a bad storm – '

'Aye, aye, 'twas,' muttered Miss McNab, beginning to close the door. But the boy, leaning on his motorbike, was happy to go on talking.

'I hope it's nae bad news in yer telegram. D'ye ken what it is?'

Hackett gritted his teeth in agitation at the delay. The cousins were desperately wondering how to signal to the boy.

'Nae, nae, I dinnae ken,' snapped Miss McNab.

'Ye read terrible things in these telegrams. Why, when me mum and dad were away,' – Hackett was turning pink with annoyance – 'me mum died an' one o' these telegrams arrived. I was so afeared, I coudnae pick it up.' The boy didn't seem to notice that Miss McNab was hovering to and fro, twitching with agitation.

But then she burst in, 'Aye, aye. Well, I'm right busy and I cannae let me cake burn, so good day tae ye.' The boy opened his mouth to speak but Miss McNab closed the door in his face, much to his astonishment, and scurried back to Hackett. The men gathered round as Hackett opened the telegram which was addressed to Finley Cox. While the men's attention was distracted from them, John and Michelle crept to the window, hoping to signal to the boy. But his back was to them as he made his way through the trees. He did not glance back at the house so they could not wave. If they knocked on the window the men would hear them. As the boy disappeared, the cousins, disappointed, turned back to the men and went to see what was in the telegram. It read:

'Yates here. Can't travel. Come to Yorkshire with Evans.

Grier'

'So,' grinned Hackett. 'A change of plans. I wonder why Yates and Grier can't make it. So tomorrow morning we'll be off to Yorkshire with the last two lockets waiting for us. I'll let the Tigress know. She can pick us up at Grier's.'

'Shouldn't we set off now?' asked Sanders.

'Nah, nah,' was the casual reply. 'Enjoy a little rest while we can.'

Cox looked explosive. The men sat down again. Puzzled and bewildered by the new plans, the cousins were still very tired and Michelle fell asleep for an hour while John sat brooding over their misfortunes. Sanders switched on the television and they watched a morning film. John and Michelle were mentioned as still being missing on the news at lunchtime. While Michelle helped Miss McNab make salad for lunch, Sebastian curled up on John's knee, purring like an engine. Hackett was in an agitated mood.

'The sight of these kids hanging about makes me sick,' he announced after lunch. 'Sanders, go and lock them in some other room. Get a key from Cox.' Miss McNab took them upstairs.

'Half the rooms in this big house are nae used nae mair. This one has a lock,' she explained, opening the door of a large disused bedroom. 'Will it do?'

'OK,' Sanders said. 'Give me the key for it.' Sebastian had followed John upstairs and slipped in just before Sanders locked the door. It was a miserable-looking room with mouldy walls, a bare-boarded floor, a small couch with a torn cover, a bed with damp, dirty bedclothes, and other odd pieces of furniture. John walked to the dusty window and peered through. There were no handy drainpipes to climb down. The nearest tree was a stout, unsteady-looking specimen, quite a distance from the window. John sighed and sank on the couch. Michelle joined him.

'My, what a brilliant holiday this is!' John said ironically. 'And now it seems we're being dragged off to Yorkshire. Huh! What fun!'

'Yes,' muttered Michelle, quiet and sad.

'Still,' reflected John with a weary sigh, 'I suppose the more they shunt us around the country,

the more chance we have of being seen and rescued.' Despite the bitterness and despair he felt, it
was a slight relief to be able to express his thoughts
without the men listening in and commenting or
snapping 'Shurrup!'

Michelle ruffled the cold fur on Sebastian's
striped forehead which was rubbing against her
ankles.

'Don't worry, John. I'm sure God will help us to
get out of all this.' John sighed again, but this time
remorsefully.

'I'm afraid I neglect my prayers,' he confessed,
'but it's now I need to say them most.' The follow-
ing pensive silence was broken by the scratching
sound of Sebastian sharpening his claws on the side
of the couch. Michelle smiled as he leapt up beside
her. He cheered them up considerably.

From time to time Sanders came to check on the
cousins. About eight o'clock he brought them mugs
of watery soup and some bread.

'What if my dad can't afford the ransom?' John
asked him. 'Will you have to kill us?'

Sanders scowled. 'Your dad will get the ransom,'
he said and stomped away. Michelle was thinking
about home. Hot tears were prickling her eyes but
she didn't want to cry in front of John. They drank
the soup and consumed the dry bread.

As the hours dragged by it grew very stuffy again.

'I hope there won't be another storm,' Michelle
said.

'On the weather forecast after the news it said
there could be thunder in the north,' John remem-

bered. The bed was too damp to get into. John lay on the couch and Michelle on top of the bed.

The storm broke in the middle of the night. The deafening peals of thunder woke Michelle. Rain was spitting fiercely on the window. She tried to get to sleep again. But suddenly she heard an eerie creaking noise. She sat up uneasily. Whatever could it be? It was coming from outside – a terrible creaking and groaning. Cautiously, she slipped off the bed and crept to the window. She caught her breath in terror. The tree opposite the window was swaying from side to side in the violent wind, creaking as it bent towards the house. A flash of lightning lit the scene and made it even more terrifying.

'John,' gasped Michelle, and then, pulling herself together, lifted her voice. 'JOHN! WAKE UP! JOHN!' Another fork of lightning ripped the dark sky, and a fraction of a second later a tremendous peal of thunder rent the air. This time the noise woke John. He grunted in discontent and rolled over, forgetting he was on a couch and not a bed. He tumbled on to the floor and cursed as his head hit the wooden boards. Now fully awake, he sat up rubbing his eyes and ruffling his blond hair as he felt his head. Michelle suddenly turned and backed hastily from the window. Her face was shiny with sweat. Speechless with horror she pointed through the window. *Creaking mournfully, the tree was falling towards the house – towards the very room they were in!* John leapt to his feet. The cousins flattened themselves against a wall as far away from the window as possible. The creaking became even louder and the tangle of branches loomed towards them. With a deafening boom some of the branches crashed through the roof. Plaster and rubble tumbled to the floor. The cousins shielded their faces with their arms as the tree came through the window, smashing it to smithereens; broken, jagged pieces of glass flew around the room, making a clatter as they hit the floor. One of them hit John's hand. He winced at the sharp pain as the blood oozed out. Above the hiss of rain, rattle of smashing glass and clatter of bits of ceiling hitting the floor was the cracking sound as twigs and branches snapped off the tree. The rain poured through the smashed window; puddles formed on the floor; water seeped through between the boards. John and Michelle surveyed the damage. Broken twigs and leaves were strewn over the drenched floor among the hundreds of splinters of glass. Massive branches stuck through the window. The wind howled and surged into the room. Michelle shivered at its cold touch. John grew excited. The tree now slanted from the window down to the ground. They could crawl down it! While John was thinking this, Michelle had just realised that a terrified Sebastian was mewing piteously in one corner of the room.

As she went to comfort him, John cried, 'Leave that cat alone! Look, we can climb down this tree to the ground. It will be easy. The tree is slanting.' Michelle was dubious. 'Never mind arguing,' persisted the impetuous John. 'Shove the bed against the door so the men can't get in. They're bound to be awake after the crash. We must escape before they get in! *Hurry up*! *Do as I say*!' Michelle didn't like his bossiness but began to ram the bed into the door, complaining at the same time.

'It could be unsafe. If the tree isn't stable you could fall off . . .'

'It's OK.' John's voice was full of excitement. 'I'll go down first to make sure it's safe. You follow. In this darkness we're unlikely to be seen. Pile stuff on the bed to make it more difficult for the men to move.'

'But – ' began Michelle, worried about her cousin's safety. However, it was no use trying to stop him. John pushed aside the flexible boughs and scrambled on to a stout branch with his stomach against the bark and his knees and arms clutching the sides of the branch. Feet first he wriggled along through the window.

'Good luck, John,' gulped an anxious Michelle.

'Thanks.' He wriggled down on his stomach, the rain pounding mercilessly on his back. The rough bark scratched his arms as he clung on. He edged his way on to the thick trunk of the tree. Now and then he stopped to pant, his hands clutching any stumps where branches had broken off. As John wriggled feet first down the slanting tree-trunk, Michelle was piling chairs on to the bed. Below, she could hear the men's agitated voices and Wagner howling. Outside John could also hear the howling. At one window he saw a torch flash. He wondered why the men were not using the lights. The electricity cable must have come down in the storm. That was a stroke of luck for the cousins, as it meant they were less likely to be seen crawling down the tree. Rain trickled over John's face. He looked down; not far now. In moments his feet would touch the mushy grass. He was anxious about Michelle. Suppose the men broke into the room while she was still there? He called up in a low voice.

'Michelle. Come down now.' Michelle went to the window. She swallowed hard. It was not far to the ground but, all the same, she didn't like the look of it. But then she heard the men's pounding footsteps on the stairs and this urged her to crawl on to the stout branch and fearfully wriggle down, clutching at the tree until her knuckles were white. Her heart was beating fast. Fear of falling and the rain running over her back made her shiver. She wanted to stay still where she was, clutching the tree-trunk with her arms and knees, eyes tightly closed; but she heard the men pounding on the door of the room and fear of being discovered made her scramble to the ground. As she paused, panting with relief, she saw Sebastian at the top of the tree, torn between the desire to follow them and the loathing of getting wet in the rain. Michelle had become attached to Miss McNab's cat and felt a little sorry at leaving him, but John was already urging her to run. The moon was hidden. It was pitch dark and they had to hold hands to avoid losing each other. All around them in the complete blackness they could hear the rain splattering on leaves and lashing down through branches, then spitting at the muddy ground and bouncing off it. Their bodies trembled in the chilly running water. Tangled roots and stones lurked on the ground in the dark, waiting to trip them up. They wound their way among trees and bushes, shivering at the peals of thunder. Their wet hair slapped in their faces, and rain hissed at them and stung their eyes. A flash of lightning let them see that they were now in an area with less trees and more muddy, heathery land. A sort of eerie mist hung near the ground. As they ran on, a cloud uncovered part of the moon, letting a trickle of light free. Suddenly, as John, who was in the lead, put his foot forward, it sank into the ground. Mud swallowed his legs up to the knees. In vain, he tried to tug out his feet.

'Don't go any further, Michelle!' John yelled. 'Stop where you are. It's a bog!'

Michelle gasped as the moonlight revealed her cousin being sucked into the mud. He felt the brown substance clinging to him from his feet to his waist. It was not too late for Michelle. She was still on firm ground. The bog spread before her. She stretched out her hand for John but couldn't reach, so she lay on her stomach on the firm ground, stretched out her arms and clutched John's hands in hers. The cruel bog was sucking in its victim. Michelle was trying desperately to pull John out, but he sank till mud reach his shoulders. Michelle was almost in tears. She couldn't let John go under, but her muscles were stretched like elastic and it seemed they would snap in two at any moment. As the bog swallowed John, Michelle was terrified that his sweaty hands would slip out of hers. John's face was white, his teeth clenched. Tears glistened in Michelle's eyes.

'Oh, John,' she moaned, 'I can't hold on much longer!'

chapter six

The Men With More Lockets

The mud was clamped round John's body.

'Let go, then,' he begged in a hoarse whisper, 'or you'll be sucked in too.'

'No, no. I can't do that either.' Both of them had the same pain of overstretched muscles in their arms. Their rainwashed faces were wrought with distress. John was praying silently.

'Please forgive me for my sins. If I die, please comfort Michelle and my parents . . .'

But Michelle's silent prayer was different.

'Please save John. Please send help . . .'

Her prayer was answered. Not far off they heard the men's voices. Michelle clung to John's hands, gathered together all the breath she had and yelled, '*Over here! Help! Over here!*' Worn out and still holding her cousin's hands she rested her aching head on the wet ground. She could hear pounding footsteps. She had never thought that she would ever be relieved to see the gang, but nothing could have pleased her more than to see Sanders, Dudgeon and Rumsey rushing to the rescue. After a long struggle, John was dragged free. Hackett looked furious. Dudgeon was exhausted, and all the men were panting; but Michelle was full of joy and relief.

Tears of happiness trickled down her muddy cheeks.

John sat on the firm ground panting. He was plastered in mud which dripped down him as if it were the wax melting on a candle and dripping down the side. He couldn't believe he was still alive! The rain began to wash off some of the mud. John felt uncomfortable in his sticky brown suit but the bliss in Michelle's face and his own relief more than made up for it. Hackett was gathering his breath to explode with fury at them. He did not enjoy getting up in the middle of the night and running around in a storm after a couple of confounded teenagers. Sanders yanked John to his feet. They began to work their way back to Cox's house. It looked dreary in the dark. The front door was wide open . . . Hackett stared as a dreadful thought struck him. He swung round, seething with anger, to face his companions.

'Which of you left that door unlocked?' It was like the voice of a madman. Michelle had never seen anyone with such a temper before. The others stopped. Sanders, Dudgeon, Coker and Rumsey were tense and silent. The hiss of rain continued. Rumsey grew pale; his ears turned pink; guilt was written all over his face. His eyes would not meet Hackett's fiery gaze. The thug turned and stamped up the steps. There was a trail of wet footprints through the hall as they trooped in. Dudgeon slammed shut the door, blocking out the hiss of the driving rain. The soaked party stood shivering in the hall as Hackett stamped up ths stairs. No one followed him. They heard him open the door of Cox's room, then trembled as a roar of fury rent the air. Hackett came to the top of the stairs, eyes bulging, teeth clenched.

'*Where is Cox?*' The dreadful voice boomed down the stairs.

Cox and Miss McNab had both gone. It was no use denying the fact after Rumsey and Dudgeon rushed round to the back of the house and found Cox's car gone, and deep tyre tracks in the mud. Miss McNab's small, battered vehicle had been left behind.

The men took John and Michelle into the dining-room. Sanders lit some candles and propped up their torches. They could not see Hackett's face as he sat brooding on the sofa; it was in darkness. They waited with dread for Hackett to erupt. Sanders was already making up calming speeches.

'Those kids,' bawled Hackett, pointing an accusing finger at the cousins, 'they're *ruining* us! We're always having to chase after them! We have to keep them out of sight and feed them and stop them escaping. *Why should we?* They're a darned nuisance!' His voice had reached a high-pitched scream. The cousins tried not to tremble. Hackett whipped out his gun and pointed it at them, his eyes burning madly, and the white candlelight flickering on his face. John swallowed hard. 'And *now*,' Hackett screamed on, 'because of *them* Cox has escaped! Well, I've had *enough*! I'm gonna get rid of these kids once and for all!' He steadied the hand which held the gun. Only John heard Michelle's terrified little gasp, and he put a comforting arm round her shoulders. They both knew Hackett wasn't joking. Sanders stood up. His hand shot out and snatched the gun.

'OK, Hackett. Calm down. Things aren't so bad. OK, Cox 'as escaped, but at least that means we don't 'ave to get rid of 'im ourselves.'

'But he'll go to the cops!' screeched Hackett.

'How can he?' reasoned Sanders. 'Cox is in trouble with the police – big trouble. He's not going to go and tell them we've nicked his locket. He's a wanted crook. And that McNab woman's just as bad. She shares his loot, and natters to people like an innocent old woman while Cox robs their houses.'

'But he'll tell Yates and Grier we're after their lockets!'

'What if he does?' replied Sanders. 'They're not going to disappear, 'cos they need the lockets *we*'ve got. They'll wait for us at Grier's, won't they? It's their only chance. Cox is probably heading there right now – that's if he doesn't come back here and try to get the lockets off us by himself. And we'll make short work of him if he does that!'

Hackett growled and produced another objection. 'He might tip off the cops about those dratted kids. The cops could be here any minute!'

'If we get arrested,' pointed out Sanders, 'that means no lockets and no jewels for Cox. There's no way he'll tip off the cops. He'd more likely come back here and try to snatch the lockets off us. Some of us'd better keep a look-out just in case.'

'I still say I've 'ad enough of those kids,' grumbled Hackett, still smouldering after his eruption. 'They're getting us into trouble all the time.'

'We'll just have to keep a closer eye on them, that's all. It was a chance in a million, that tree coming down. Besides, if you don't want fifty thousand quid, I do.'

'I'd rather lose the ransom than lose those jewels,' Hackett declared.

'We can have both, if we're smart.'

'Aw, give over. You're just trying to shield those kids. There may be *some* sense in what you say, but gimme my gun. I won't shoot 'em now. I'll wait and see if I need to.' Hackett gave the cousins a menacing look and turned back to Sanders. 'Rumsey and Coker can go and keep a look-out for Cox. You and Dudgeon can take over in a couple of hours, till it's light. The kids are gonna sleep in here with us, and we'll be off first thing in the morning. I was thinking we'd borrow Cox's motor, but now I s'pose we'll 'ave to use that lorry. It's going to be risky.'

'We could use the old lady's car,' piped up Coker, trying to look intelligent.

'Aw, sure!' sneered Hackett in crushing tones. 'So long as half of us sit in the boot! That's if you can open the door without the thing falling to pieces!' The crestfallen Coker coloured in embarrassment.

'At least we could switch the number-plates from 'er car,' pointed out Sanders, 'seeing that the lorry's nicked and the cops'll be looking out for it.'

'Yeh,' agreed Hackett, annoyed that he hadn't thought of the idea himself. 'You can go and do it before you go to sleep.'

'Big deal,' muttered Sanders, striding out.

'Are you gonna phone the Tigress on the way and tell 'er wot's 'appened?' Rumsey asked cautiously. Hackett scowled. The prospect didn't delight him.

'Shurrup! I'll see! You and Coker better get outside and keep your eyes peeled for Cox!' The men departed, grumbling in low voices.

Hackett stretched out on the couch, while Dudgeon sprawled in an armchair. The exhausted cousins dropped off to sleep on a rug and both had nightmares. Michelle dreamt that she was clinging to the tree – almost falling off. At the window above her was the terrible face of Hackett, twice more ugly and angry than in real life, yelling, 'Where's Cox?' Then she fell off the tree and was trying to pull John out of the bog. For ages she went through agonies, trying not to let him go under. Then the person in the bog was a glaring Hackett but she couldn't let go of him . . . John tossed and turned with a wet brow as he relived the terror of being sucked into the bog. The mud closed over his head and he was falling, falling . . . Suddenly there was a sharp pain in his side, and he woke with a yelp of surprise to find himself still in Cox's house. It was dawn and cigarette smoke swam round the room. All the nightmares had gone but the pain in his side was still there. He looked up and saw Hackett, who had just kicked him in the ribs to wake him up. John slowly rose to his feet. He looked around. Rumsey and Coker were still snoring.

'Wake up those sloths!' Hackett said to Sanders. 'I've thought of something I want to tell you.' He spread a road map out on the table. Five dishevelled heads bent over it. Hackett asked quite cheerfully, 'Any of you remember Maxie MacPherson?' Four blank faces stared at him. 'Surely you remember old Maxie? Two years ago – red-haired guy – car-dealer – '

'Oh, yeh,' burst in Sanders as light dawned suddenly. 'That feller we did the Newcastle job with?' Hackett nodded and placed a fat fingertip on the road map.

'And he lived somewhere around here. I don't like going round in this nicked lorry, even with the new number-plates. We'll borrow a better motor from Maxie on our way ter Yorkshire. An' another thing.' He rounded on John. 'We've ter contact yer dad. I've planned it all.'

It seemed that Cox had not turned up during the night. After a rapid breakfast the gang and the cousins climbed into the farm lorry. Outside it was cloudy but not raining. Sanders drove across the dewy grass on to the road. In the back of the lorry, the cousins were sickened not to be able to see anything. They could only sense the lorry driving along a bumpy road and wet branches brushing on the roof. Michelle wondered what had happened to Sebastian and Wagner. Tired, uncomfortable in wet clothes, longing for home and coughing on Dudgeon's cigarette smoke, the cousins had no idea how long they were in the back of the vehicle. But after what seemed hours of jolting up and down in darkness, misery and discomfort, Sanders brought the lorry to a halt. When Dudgeon opened the back to get out, John and Michelle saw a squalid garage which sold second-hand cars. Near the doorway was a man of medium height in oil-smeared overalls. The top of his head was pink and bald, but there were tufts of flame-orange hair round his flabby ears. Happily for John and Michelle, Coker left the door of the back of the lorry open a crack. It was delightful to breathe in fresh air and see light, although the smell of petrol wasn't too pleasant. They crouched down, peering through the door. There was no chance of escaping; Hackett and his men were too near.

'Hi, Maxie!' called Hackett, approaching the man in overalls. He stared at Hackett with a puzzled frown. 'Remember me? Your old friend, Hackett.' A wave of recognition crossed Maxie MacPherson's face.

'Oh, aye,' he said, not very enthusiastically, fingering a spanner.

John glanced at Michelle. Briefly they exchanged weak smiles and watched to see Hackett's next move.

'I hope he doesn't shoot him,' whispered Michelle, but Hackett was taking a wad of notes out – the ones he had stolen from Cox. He waved them before Maxie's fat nose.

'We wanna borrow a motor – plenty of room inside.'

105

'I don't hire 'em. You'll 'ave to buy.'

'Nah, nah. We wanner *borrow*.' Sanders and Dudgeon closed in on a very worried-looking Maxie MacPherson.

'Well – well – 'ow long for?' he faltered uneasily.

'Oh, just a couple of days,' remarked Hackett casually. 'We'll give yer fifty quid.'

'Fifty quid! Ye're jokin'. Fifty quid my foot!' His head dropped as the three thugs closed in on him. His lips were pale. 'Well,' he muttered, 'on second thoughts, make it seventy.'

Hackett shook his head. 'Fifty.'

'Well, wait a minute.' Maxie held up his hands. 'We 'aven't even decided what ye're 'avin'. There's this old Mini.'

'Bah,' Hackett bawled. 'We don't want a tiny bashed-up old thing like that! We'll have that Dormobile thing.'

'Nay, nay!' exclaimed Maxie. 'Ye cannae have that!'

'C'me on! It's an ancient thing. You don't need it. I'll give you seventy-five quid for it – just for the loan!'

'Well,' began Maxie uneasily, 'I dinnae ken . . . Aye, all right!'

Hackett tossed some notes at Maxie and examined the Dormobile. It was cream-coloured and scratched, but spacious.

'The two back seats open oot so there's room for two folks on each,' explained MacPherson.

'Good. Keys!' snapped Hackett. 'We'll leave you this lorry.'

'Where did ye get it?' demanded Maxie suspiciously.

'Nicked it. You'll have to get rid o' it!'

'What! Now look – ' began MacPherson, but Sanders shoved him to one side.

'Aw shurrup,' he muttered. 'You're just as crooked!'

Dudgeon fetched the cousins and they were bundled into the back of the Dormobile. As he caught sight of them, a look of surprise crossed MacPherson's face.

'Oh, by the way, Maxie,' remarked Hackett, 'not a word to anyone that you've seen us – or we might remember that little job you did with us!' He and Sanders clambered into the front, while Rumsey opened out the two back seats, forming two short cushioned benches. Rumsey and Coker sat on one and Michelle had to sit next to Dudgeon on the other. John squatted on a blanket on the floor. So that the cousins couldn't be seen, Sanders told Rumsey to draw all the curtains in the back, but John and Michelle could now see where they were going through the large windscreen at the front. They left a worried-looking Maxie MacPherson shaking his head and fingering his money. As the Dormobile engine sang contentedly, the cousins surveyed the surrounding scenery. Grass wavered in fields and buttercups stretched from the roadsides. Beyond trees festooned with green frills rose smooth hill slopes dappled with sunlight.

Anyone who has spent hours in a cramped car devoid of all amusement will begin to understand

107

how the cousins felt – and worry and the presence of the five men made it even worse. John felt sick crouching on the floor. Michelle was very uncomfortable; there was a bit of metal on the window which kept jabbing her in the back. They both grew very hungry and thirsty. Coker muttered something about lunch and was ignored at the time, but later Sanders stopped the vehicle in a tiny village and bought some stale rolls and hamburgers from a dingy, deserted café.

When they had devoured the food inside the Dormobile, Sanders told Hackett, 'There's a callbox here, and it's about time.'

'OK. You and Dudgeon bring the kid,' Hackett ordered, opening a door. Michelle pursed her lips angrily as Dudgeon roughly grabbed John and pulled him out on to the dusty sun-scorched road. There was no one around, and a scratched red telephone box stood at the roadside. John could feel a gun pressed against his ribs as he was hustled inside.

'Right,' Hackett snarled, 'you'll dial your home number. If your dad doesn't answer, you say 'I want to speak to Mr Lester' – nothing more. Don't answer *any* questions! When your dad comes you say this: "Dad, this is John. I'm all right. The kidnappers want fifty thousand pounds. They're giving you a week to get it. We'll contact you later." You say nothing more. You don't answer any questions' – the gun dug painfully into his side – 'because if you say one false word . . .' The unfinished sentence was more effective than a completed threat. Wild ideas were rushing through John's head. The men were crafty not speaking themselves. But could he phone someone else and deliver Hackett's speech? Still, what good would that do? They wouldn't understand him and, even if they did, wouldn't be able to do anything that his father couldn't. Even if the police answered the phone and traced the call, they would be gone in the Dormobile before any policemen arrived there.

Reluctantly John dialled the number of his home. It was answered immediately by his father.

'Hello, Dad, this is John,' began the boy apprehensively, aware of Hackett's steely eye on him. Mr Lester broke in before John could continue.

'John, where are you? What – ?'

'I'm all right. Um – er – the kidnappers want fifty thousand pounds. You've to get it in – em – a week. They'll contact you later – '

'John, are you hurt? What about Michelle? Have they harmed you . . .?' The flow of anxious questions flooded out. John eyed Hackett, who glared at him as if to say, 'That's enough.'

'Goodbye,' broke in John unhappily, and, suddenly overcome with emotion, gasped, 'I'm sorry, Dad!' and put down the receiver. He turned to face Hackett, wondering what he would say about the last words. Hackett just glared and bundled John into the back of the Dormobile. The engine roared. John sighed and threw back his head, staring through the roof window at the blue silk sky, miserably. He could tell by his father's voice that their families were suffering no less than the cousins. The day was hot and the sun fired its rays at the Dormobile. Michelle had a roaring headache which made her feel ill. Both cousins felt rather sick. The unpleasant smell of petrol fumes didn't make them feel any better.

The journey and the day seemed never-ending. It was about five o'clock when the Dormobile reached Yorkshire. Blue rivers glistened in the sun, bordered with rocks and fresh green grass. Patchworks of fields, golden, olive, green and yellow, stretched for miles. Cows, with flies buzzing round them, chewed the long grass with all the time in the world, and ponies rested soft muzzles on rickety fences of gnarled wood, staring at passing vehicles through placid brown eyes. Birds fluttered among the treetops and sheep dotted the gentle hill slopes. Golden fingers of sunlight stretched over stone dykes and fields; bumpy roads crossed crumbling bridges over merrily gurgling streams in which cattle stood lazily, sipping, chewing and swishing their tails, with the cool water running over their hot flanks. The hazy blue sky, quivering violet foxgloves, fields powdered with daisies and the tips of grass blades glinting in the sunlight added to the rugged beauty.

It was not until six o'clock that the Dormobile reached its destination – a lonely farm. Sanders drove up a lane to the farmhouse. The men talked in low voices and then Hackett announced, 'The kids can walk in front. They might be armed. That should stop them if they're waiting to fire at us from inside the house.'

'Oh, great!' snorted John. 'So now we act as firing targets!' He was ignored and they all clambered out, the men glancing around cautiously. There was no sign of anyone in the farmhouse as they strode somewhat stiffly to the door with the cousins in the lead. Hackett and Sanders were clutching their guns. Some hens were strutting around, preening their feathers as they paraded before the doorstep. The birds flew upwards in a squawking cloud of red feathers and flapping wings, protesting in an extravagant cacophony as the men and cousins strode into their midst to reach the front door. Hackett hesitated, then savagely kicked it so that it slowly swung open. He gripped his revolver and they listened. A clink of china cups was audible. The men barged in, charged through the hall, pushing the cousins in front of them, and invaded a homely sitting-room. The bright reds and oranges gave it a warm and welcoming feeling. At the table, standing with his back to them, a small stout man, with his right arm in a sling, was awkwardly pouring tea from a steaming brown teapot. He wore dirty jeans tucked into grubby wellington boots, and had shrivelled horny brown skin and fingernails black with dirt. As he heard footsteps he swung round, his shaggy eyebrows shooting up. The face was bitter and shrew-like, and looked as if it had been carelessly moulded out of sticky wax, leaving creases, a couple of warts and unusually large bags under the little black boot-button eyes, which were stamped in close together beneath a protruding brow. The distrustful eyes stared hard at the men, and the thin, dry lips, which seemed to have been drained of all ruddiness, were still, and seemed no more than a lifeless slot cut above the blue pointed chin. With a bony hand he smoothed his dome-shaped mop of grey hair, which was without a parting, and the lips twitched unwillingly.

'What?' The voice was quick and piercing, as he caught sight of Hackett's gun.

'Hello, Grier,' Hackett boomed with an ugly, toothy grin, which displayed smugness and satisfaction. Grier hesitated.

'Who are you and what are you doing here?' The words were spat out and the high-pitched voice bore a Yorkshire accent.

'Where's Yates? And Cox – isn't he here yet?' Grier looked perplexed and a puzzled line crinkled his forehead.

'Cox? I wish he *was* here. I'm expecting him with a friend, but I don't know where he's got to. Why are *you* so interested? What has this – ?'

'So he hasn't even phoned you!' interrupted Hackett, with a puzzled glance at Sanders. 'Anyway, where's Yates?'

'Oh, him. He's in t' kitchen.'

'Well, get him, then!' Grier strolled to the door. 'Yates! Come in here.'

'Wha' for?' demanded an unfriendly voice, and feet thundered on the floor as a very annoyed-looking young man stomped into the room. His thin blond hair was combed into greasy strands and a short, bristly moustache adorned the screwed-

112

up face which was made unpleasant with scowl lines.

'Wha's going on?' He stopped short as his eyes fell on Hackett's revolver.

'I wish I knew!' Grier sounded bewildered and agitated. He turned to Hackett. 'Perhaps you'll explain.'

'Yes, who are you?' Yates demanded very grumpily.

'First things first. We'd rather like your lockets.' Both men started and exchanged glances.

'Wha' lockets?' Yates growled.

'Tut, tut! Don't play the little innocent 'un with me.' Hackett's voice turned menacing. 'This gun is loaded!' When they hesitated slightly he scowled. 'I'll give you three seconds. One, two – '

'OK. They're in that cigar-box on the sideboard.'

'Take a look, Dudgeon,' Hackett said. Dudgeon flicked open the lid of the cigar-box and lifted out four fat brown cigars.

'False bottom,' Grier said. Dudgeon fiddled about in the box and lifted the false bottom.

'They're here,' he smirked, pulling out the twinkling lockets. 'Both of 'em.'

'Good. Bring them here.' As he laid his gun on the table in order to examine the lockets, he told Sanders, 'You cover them.' Hackett smirked as he gloated over the silver jewellery.

'So you've still to get the other two lockets?' Grier said.

'I already have them.' It was obvious that he enjoyed uttering that smug sentence.

'Oh *sure* you have!' mocked Yates disbelievingly. 'Off Cox and Evans? Bah!'

'Yeh, off Cox and Evans.' Hackett, with a superior air, produced the other two lockets and spread all four on his ugly palm. He leered, and Sanders indicated the settee to Yates, Grier and the cousins. Hackett waited until the four were squeezed on to the sofa and sneered, 'I'm afraid you won't see Evans again, nor any of the lockets, and it doesn't look as though you'll be seeing Cox again either.'

'And that's just where you're wrong, my dear Hackett!' a voice boomed round the room, and in the doorway loomed the bulky form of a triumphant Cox, the pink head shining in the light from the hallway, the bristly beard framing a flashing white grin and the right forefinger round the trigger of a black rifle! '*Drop that gun*, Sanders!'

Taken unawares, Sanders's jaw dropped and he stared at the threatening rifle muzzle. Slowly his fingers unfolded and reluctantly he tossed his gun on to the carpet. Yates and Grier began sniggering. Hackett's hand moved towards his revolver on the table.

'Don't touch that!' warned Cox, then emitted a gruff chortle. 'Ha! You fell into our trap easily. I see you've kindly gathered all the lockets together for us, Hackett, just as we planned! How nice! Now what was that someone mentioned about me seeing the last of the jewels? Now lay the lockets on – '

At that moment Dudgeon, who was standing nearest, hurled himself at Cox, trying to seize the rifle. The weapon went off with a violent bang and smoke rose from its tip, while the bullet was whizzing straight towards the cousins!

chapter seven

The Hidden Message

As soon as John saw Dudgeon leaping at Cox, sensing the danger he had pushed Michelle off the couch to safety and tried to duck himself. But he had hardly moved before the bullet whizzed through his shirtsleeve, grazing his arm, and ploughed into the back of the couch. At the same time Dudgeon was overpowering an infuriated Cox, and, after snatching his rifle, covered his opponent with it. Meanwhile Sanders, pushing aside Grier, who was eagerly scrabbling on the floor, retrieved his revolver and ordered Yates, who had leapt up to try to snatch Hackett's gun, to retire to the couch. The two conquered men sank back flabbergasted, and Sanders covered them while Hackett turned his attention to Cox, who was pink in the face and incensed with rage.

'Tough luck, ole feller,' jeered Hackett, sweeping the four lockets into his voluminous pocket. 'Now – just stay there and don't move. Huh! You didn't think you could get the better of *me*?' he chortled, as if it was he who had saved the situation rather than Dudgeon.

Michelle had scrambled to her feet and was anxiously looking at her cousin, who was clutching his arm and resisting the urge to dance about in pain.

'Oh, stop moaning!' snarled Hackett. 'And keep still – you've not been shot!'

'It grazed me,' John said.

'Oh *dear*!' mocked Hackett nastily, and then snapped, 'Can't you stop hopping from one foot to the other and clutching your arm?'

'Perhaps,' suggested John bitterly, 'you'd like me to fire at *you* with the rifle – then you can give us a demonstration of how to do so.'

'Shurrup and sit down, or you won't just have a grazed arm,' Hackett threatened, and then turned to Grier and Yates, who were grumbling at Cox.

'So much for your brainwave of a plan!' Grier was complaining.

'Shurrup,' snapped Hackett, and indicated Grier's sling. 'Is that why you couldn't drive to Cox's?'

'Yes,' snapped Grier, with bitter, flashing eyes.

'What about you?' Hackett asked of Yates. 'Why couldn't you drive?'

Yates pouted and played with his fingers, his eyes bright with anger and discomfort.

'Why?' boomed Hackett.

Yates squirmed and looked embarrassed. A smirk crept on to Hackett's face.

'Ha! It's because you *can't* drive, isn't it?' he jeered.

Yates swallowed and snorted angrily.

'*Isn't it?*' Hackett repeated, cold and menacing.

117

'Yes,' Yates growled in a voice barely audible. Hackett snorted in contempt.

'So how'd you get here? Hitch-hiked?'

Yates emitted a grunt of assent and Hackett turned and cast a superior smirk on the smouldering Cox.

'You haven't got that wretched dog with you, have you?' he asked casually, with a gruff chuckle.

'Wagner ran out into the rain during the storm,' muttered Cox, unable to conceal deep regret. 'That's the last I saw of him.'

'Aw, poor Cox has lost his doggy!' mocked Hackett. 'Not to mention his locket! Well, I've a phone-call to make.'

The cousins wondered who Hackett was going to ring. The Tigress perhaps? They were determined to overhear the conversation. While Hackett went into the hall, Sanders continued to cover the prisoners. His eyes wandered to the teapot and he nodded at Yates.

'Get us some tea.'

Yates grudgingly arose and crossed to the table. The cousins also stood up and moved seats nearer the door. Sanders eyed them suspiciously but didn't seem to mind. They heard the whirr of the telephone dial and then Hackett spoke.

'Hackett here. We're at Grier's place. Yates an' Cox are here too ... Yeh, all four now ... What? Yeh, well, it's a long story ... OK ... Yeh ... Not yet ... Oh! Well, I thought you'd want to know what was going on ... Yeh. OK. We'll do it now ... Yeh, course I've still got it ... Oh, it's in my wallet . . . Well, it's safe enough there . . . Oh, well, mebbe not, but I've still got it . . . OK . . . in an hour or so . . .'

The phone tinkled as he laid down the receiver. He strode back into the room and thoughtfully looked at Grier, Yates and Cox.

'Sanders, stop slurping tea. Go and see if there's a place we can lock these three up out of the way.'

Sanders strode out and shortly returned to announce that there was a cellar, twirling the key between his fingers.

'OK, give Rumsey your gun,' Hackett instructed him. 'Dudgeon, take Rumsey – and Coker – and lock those three in the cellar.' Grier, Yates and Cox were ushered out of the room. 'We've ter do the code,' Hackett announced. The cousins pricked up their ears.

'Aren't you gonna get the kids out too?' asked Sanders.

'No, they're staying here. I want to keep an eye on them myself. Anyway, it doesn't matter if they know where we're going. They'll be going there with us soon enough anyhow.'

Hackett and Sanders strode to the table. Hackett turned the four silver lockets out of his pocket. They glistened on the wooden surface. John moved over to the table followed by Michelle. The men didn't appear to notice. Hackett was taking out a leather wallet from inside his jacket. He thumbed through it and took out a folded piece of lined paper. This he opened out and laid on the table. The paper bore rows of strange symbols, each one with a letter of the alphabet marked beside it – symbols similar, if not identical, to those engraved on the fronts of the lockets. Was the pretty engraving on each locket really a piece of code?

'Poor old Webb!' sniggered Sanders. 'If only he knew his innocent little sister had nicked some of his code papers!'

'Hmm. Got a pen and paper?' Hackett asked.

'Might have.' Sanders produced a Biro with a chewed end and tore a piece of blank paper out of the front of a book on Grier's sideboard. The men sat down. Hackett glanced up and scowled at the cousins.

'What're you staring at?' he demanded.

'The code,' John answered casually. 'It's frightfully interesting, you know.'

'Shurrup!' Hackett said, glaring. 'Go an' sit on that couch.'

Reluctantly they obeyed. While Hackett was examining the lockets, Dudgeon, Rumsey and Coker thundered back into the room.

'Boy, could I do with a drink!' groaned Rumsey.

'And could I do with some grub!' whimpered Coker, rubbing his stomach.

'Aw, shurrup an' sit down,' Hackett ordered. 'The Tigress says ter do the code.'

'Oh! So that's why we had to take Cox and Yates and Grier out!' exclaimed Coker, looking as stupid as ever.

'*Sit down!*' snapped Hackett. The five heads bent over the lockets and list of symbols. Hackett chewed the end of the Biro and scrawled on the paper torn from the book. The cousins were desperate to see what was going on, but they had to be content to listen to squabbling, letters being read aloud and gruff voices protesting, 'That's wrong. You do it sideways!' or 'Don't be stupid! That doesn't make sense!' After what seemed hours and hours but was really only just over thirty minutes, Hackett sat back frowning and held up his scrap of paper which was covered in scored out letters.

'Hmm.' He seemed rather perturbed. 'So, *Falcon's Head Rock, Falake Fjord, Norway.* I wasn't reckoning on going abroad. Wonder what the Tigress'll say about having to take the kids all the way to Norway! Don't reckon she'll like it much!'

'What's Falcon's Head Rock?' demanded Rumsey. 'A town?'

Hackett shrugged. 'A rock, I should think.'

'It could be a kind of rock formation in the shape of a falcon's head,' piped up John.

'Aw, keep quiet, Mr Brainbox!' snapped Hackett, and turned back to his companions. 'I'll phone the Tigress.'

While he dialled, the cousins were turning over in their minds the idea of going to Norway. They had never imagined the lockets to bear a code and wondered who had made them and how the jewels fitted into the picture. But they quickly turned their attention to Hackett on the phone.

'Yeh, it's Hackett . . . Yeh, we've done the code . . . Here's a surprise for you. It says *Falcon's Head Rock, Falake Fjord, Norway* . . . What? . . . *Tonight!* That's a bit soon . . . Well, what time will you get here . . .? But where can you land . . .? Yeh, it's a farm . . . There's a big field here – yeh – about – well, ten acres . . . Yeh, it's pretty level . . . Lights . . .? Well, we could, I s'pose, OK . . . I think there is . . . It'll have to . . . OK . . . Well, if you think you can do it . . . Well, I don't like it, but OK . . . OK.' Hackett strode back into the room, rolled his eyes to the ceiling and gave a low whistle.

'Well?' demanded Sanders and Dudgeon together.

'She's going to land tonight. We've gotter get lights set up in the field.'

'Lights? What lights? Where?' asked Sanders.

'In the big field outside. We've to use car head-lights – four lights at each end, she said.'

'We haven't got four cars,' Rumsey objected.

'There's our motor, and Cox's and Grier's must be about somewhere – and there's got to be a farm truck or something hanging around.'

'S'pose so,' muttered Sanders. 'We best get busy. And we're taking off tonight?'

'Yes.' Hackett gave out orders for the prepara-tion for the plane landing. The cousins presumed it must be a private plane belonging to the Tigress. They were to be left in the house with Coker – and Sanders's revolver. John knew that he could prob-ably overpower the cowardly Coker, but not when Coker had a gun – and also he did not want Mich-elle to get hurt. So while Coker settled down with a newspaper, a cup of tea and the revolver, the cousins knelt by the window and watched the other men breaking down a fence at the end of the field

122

just in case the plane overshot. Dusk was falling. The men drove the Dormobile, two cars and a farm truck to the fields, set them in position and tested the headlights. Then they stomped back into the room, with hot faces, plucking splinters of wood from their hands. Coker fetched some beer from the fridge, and then Sanders took Michelle into the kitchen and told her to boil some eggs and butter some bread, but the men complained that she had boiled the eggs too hard. After the hasty supper it was quite dark.

'Won't be long now,' Hackett said, looking at his watch. The minutes ticked away, and soon Coker was left behind again to guard the cousins. The four other men stepped outside where the dark velvet sky was sprinkled with twinkling stars. They crossed the fields and switched on all the headlights. The beams stretched across the ground, bleaching the grass. The cousins stifled yawns as they watched through the window. At last they heard the purr of an engine which grew louder until it drowned all other sounds. A small single-engined plane slowly descended and entered the pool of light cast by the headlamps as it touched the ground with a shudder. It ran along the improvised runway, the purr of the engine petering out. When it had stopped, a figure stepped out and the four men gathered round. Then they switched off the car headlights and all came towards the house. The cousins moved towards the doorway preparing to meet the leader of their captors, the Tigress.

chapter eight

Falcon's Head Rock

The front door swung open and footsteps sounded in the hall. The men entered the sitting-room, led by the Tigress. The cousins stared at her. So this was the evil person behind all the gang's devilish schemes! Tall and slim, the Tigress was probably in her early thirties. The cruel curves of her pale face were as smooth as if they had been carved by the most dexterous of sculptors. A golden-orange flick of hair swept across her sloping forehead, and the hollow-cheeked face, white as a ghost's, was framed by a fire-coloured mane of hair which curled under at the tips around the bottom of her slim neck. The only colours marking her face were the clear-cut outlines of her unsmiling lips, emphasised by carefully applied red gloss lipstick, and the curves of misty blue eye-shadow above the false eyelashes which shielded her pale green eyes. These cold piercing eyes scanned the room and filled the atmosphere with a kind of tension and uneasiness. Waves of efficiency and pride seemed to stream from her and an air of superiority and disgust for inferiors hung about her. Some might have declared her beautiful, but Michelle thought her features were spoiled by the evil way her cheeks curved and the lack of smile lines. She was fashionably dressed in burgundy cords with a matching gold-buttoned waistcoat over a white blouse. Her strong-smelling perfume soon scented the room. The high heels of her leather boots clicked on the floor as she entered, haughtily surveyed the room and then glanced at the cousins with considerable distaste.

Turning to Hackett, she said in dignified tones, 'I suggest we leave soon after 3 a.m.'

'If you say so,' agreed Hackett, and then told Coker to fetch some food. The Tigress looked round again.

'You told me,' she went on, 'that Yates, Grier *and* Cox were here. I presume that they are safely locked up.'

'Yeh, they're in the cellar,' Hackett told her.

'Good. We'll leave them locked in there. They don't know where we're going, and they are unlikely to be found before we have completed our business. I also presume,' she continued with a nod at John and Michelle, 'that those two know nothing of our plans.'

'Well – em – ' faltered Hackett. She cast upon him a stony gaze.

'You did get them out of the room whenever you discussed our business?'

'Er – well – actually, we had to keep an eye on them. You see, they nearly escaped once – '

'Of course, when *you* are in charge of them!' Hackett's face clouded with annoyance. 'So they were with you when you discussed the secret of the lockets,' went on the Tigress, 'and know our destination?'

'Well, I was planning to take them with us,' explained Hackett.

'And after that I suppose you were going to release them, when they have all this information!' stormed the woman.

'Does it matter if we do?' reasoned Sanders. 'As soon as we've got the ransom and let them go, we're going to disappear. They won't know where we're going or where we're taking the jewels.'

'Still, it might be safer to – ' Hackett began in a low voice, as the cousins froze. The Tigress frowned.

'*Not* if you're going to go about it the way you did with Evans! You're too irresponsible for anything Hackett! I can't even trust you to look after two children. It seems they have almost escaped, and goodness knows what else. We shall take them to Norway. Then at least I can keep my eye on them. It shouldn't take too long. They might even be some use to us – if I pass them off as my children, we shall look more like tourists. After we've got the jewels, I don't care how you release them. I shall be away before you get the ransom and return them to their parents. You assured me that you could handle it, Hackett.'

'I *can* handle it,' growled the insulted thug.

'I'm glad to hear it.' Just then Coker returned with a pot of tea and some snacks. 'I'm not surprised that my brother chose Norway,' went on the Tigress, delicately biting into a sandwich. 'He has been there a great deal and has several contacts there. I often went with him when we were children and had to go there last year. I know the area of

126

the Falake Fjord quite well, though I have never heard of the Falcon's Head Rock. There is some flat ground behind the fjord mountains – excellent for landing.'

Later on, the Tigress advised the cousins to get some sleep. When Rumsey woke them it was three o'clock in the morning. By torchlight they left Grier's farmhouse and trooped to the plane. A cool breeze licked their faces. When everyone was squeezed inside the aircraft, the Tigress started the engine. Soon they were soaring above a mass of black shapes which seemed to be sprinkled with orange and white glitter. A maze of tiny lights was punched into an inky black background. Hot and tired, the cousins dropped to sleep. When they woke, yawning, stretching and rubbing their eyes, the light was pale grey. Below them was the sea, glistening in the sunlight. Before long the coast of Norway was in sight. The Tigress studied a map closely and circled in the air.

'The Falake Fjord,' she yelled over the burr of the engine, nodding downwards. The glinting blue water was framed with bulky mountains. Some flat ground came into sight and the plane slowly descended. With a violent jerk it touched down and slid across the field, stopping near the shelter of some trees. The engine choked to silence and the pilot and passengers jumped out, the wind ruffling their hair. The Tigress explained that the Falake Fjord was not too large. They would cover it in the day, looking for the Falcon's Head Rock which she believed to be a rock formation in the form of a falcon's head. However, she said, they could make enquiries at villages. She took a flight-bag out of the plane and slung it on her shoulder.

'Wot about food?' Coker wanted to know. The Tigress gave him a withering look.

Then she turned to Hackett, saying, 'Of course, we shall be travelling by vehicle – we have a long journey over the mountains.'

'What, nick one?' Hackett asked. The Tigress glared at him.

'You seem to forget, Hackett, that this organisation has always been successful because of its efficient leader and all the arrangements being made beforehand. We – *I* do not leave things to the last minute. I have carefully arranged everything. I phoned an acquaintance, who assisted me when I was last here, and had him take care of our means of transport. Efficiency, Hackett, is what we *must* have.'

John smirked as Hackett scowled without replying. The authority the Tigress held over him was very obvious. The woman consulted a map while the cousins took in their surroundings. Nearby were the mountains, shaggy with vegetation. They all trooped towards them, leaving the plane partly concealed by trees. In places, the sky was congested with white clouds. Before long, with aching feet, they reached a small village squeezed into a nook at the foot of a mountain. The houses of slatted wood in yellow, white and pink with sloping roofs cast shade over the hot grey brick road. The odour of salt water hung in the air. The sunlight warmed their faces as the rays skimmed over the dazzling white snowcaps and spread in all their golden glory over the village. The houses were scattered here and there with the mountains looming behind them. As they were led through the streets the cousins noticed down-quilts hanging out of some windows and bicycles whizzing by. The Tigress stopped at a brightly painted white house in much the same style as the others in the street and climbed the four white steps. She rapped on the wooden door and the next instant a good-looking, brown-armed young man, tall and fair and smelling of tobacco, stood before them.

'Hello, Bergslien,' said the Tigress. The man smiled.

'You want the Falcon's Head Rock?'

'*And* transport.'

Bergslien smiled again, closed the door and trotted down the steps. They followed him to a sunny street lined with shops where tourists wandered and the buzz of chatter reigned. In a quieter part of the street Bergslien showed them a dark blue van which had windows at the back. He handed the keys to the Tigress, then took her map and pointed with his finger.

'The Falcon's Head Rock juts out over the northern end of the fjord. You follow winding roads over the mountains, then come to this village. If you are not sure ask there. A little farther on you will find the rock.' Bergslien merged into the crowd of holidaymakers while the cousins were bundled into the van. It shook as the Tigress started the engine and

129

before long they had reached the foot of a road leading up into the knobbly mountains which hid the fjord. On the lower slopes sheep were grazing, wearing bells round their necks. The road was a dirt track and quite narrow. The higher they got the more magnificent were the views. Clear mountain lakes glinted like silver, streams busily churned downwards, and steep paths wound through woods. Blue and shadowy mountains in the distance looked like huge carelessly modelled lumps of clay, powdered with snow and worn with forked grooves where streams had cut into the rock. One could see that the closer mountains were scarred and scraped, looking in places as if a giant had idly doodled and hacked at them with a huge penknife. After a while, between peaks dappled with snow, they caught glimpses of the Falake Fjord, a gorgeous blue, dotted with yachts and rowing-boats, shimmering in the sunlight and rippling the mountains' reflections.

'We will be going over the mountains, then downwards until we reach the village Bergslien spoke of,' the Tigress explained. 'There we will ask for further directions.'

The road, still winding up, was full of hairpin bends so that the blue vehicle jolted considerably as it swung from side to side. But in many places, instead of curving round the side of a massive rock, the road was tunnelled right through. The tunnel walls were often cracked and damp where melted snow had seeped down. As they were driven higher, snow formed a humped carpet on the slopes and great white walls stretched up and up on each side of the road. Sometimes the road itself was buried and sticks had been stuck into the snow to mark out the route. It was alarming to see that in places these sticks had been carried over the cliff by sliding snow. Michelle admired the view as they began going down the other side of the mountain towards the fjord. A holiday in Norway was what she had always dreamed of, but she had never planned to spend it with six wanted criminals. If only she, John and her parents were the only people in the van, spending a holiday in Norway! But, no – her parents were far, far away . . .

The Tigress drove into the village they had been heading for. It was bigger than the last but still had houses of slatted wood. It was a busier place, full of cheerful voices. Cars lined the roadside and dogs and small children ran around, getting in everyone's way. In a wider street edged with trees, hippies and salesmen had laid out squares of coloured cloth on the pavement and covered them in jewellery. People stopped to buy sparkling bracelets, gold chains and shimmering necklaces. In a quieter street the Tigress pulled up next to a yellow house where an old Norwegian man was leaning against the wall. His face was crinkled and weatherbeaten and his brown skin contrasted with his white hair. The sparkle in his eyes suggested that he enjoyed life tremendously and had many a story to tell. The Tigress stepped down from the van and approached him, leaving a window open slightly so that the others could hear. The old man grinned

131

and bade the Tigress good morning.

She returned the greeting, then asked, 'I wonder if you could tell me where I can find the Falcon's Head Rock. We're British tourists and my children here' – indicating the cousins in the van – 'heard about the rock and are dying to see it for some reason.' She spoke merrily with an ingratiating smile. The old man gave a toothy grin and nodded.

'Ah, yes, I know the Falcon's Head Rock. But it is nothing spectacular – an interesting rock formation perhaps, but there are better things to see in Norway. Show your children the stave church at Borgund; take them to the Viking Ships Museum to see the famous *Oseberg*, or to the Parliament Building – it is a lovely sight; and there are wonderful pictures in the Town Hall.'

'Thank you, but we have seen most of these things,' lied the Tigress. 'Now, the Fa-'

'But have you been to Bergen? It is a very interesting town – and beautiful. You will see there the old merchant houses from the thirteenth to seventeenth centuries. In Bergen they sell herring and have many other fish. In many places the air smells of fish. Take your children to Drammen to see the magnificent spiral. There is no other like it – and what about the silver mines in Kongsberg? It is cold in the tunnels but – '

In the van Hackett was seething with impatience, but, if the Tigress was becoming at all annoyed with waiting, she hid it beautifully.

'Thank you,' she said. 'I am sure we will visit all these places. But as the children are so keen to see the rock and as we are, I understand, quite near it, I would be grateful if you give us some directions.'

'Of course,' grinned the loquacious old man.

'I have a map.'

'Ah, good.' While their heads were bent over the map, their voices were not so clear, but soon the Tigress was back in the van.

'Look out for trolls!' called the man as they drove off. 'They are supposed to live in the mountains.' He chuckled.

The cousins spotted glaciers crawling down the mountainsides, which had been scratched and scarred by ice in many places. The road wound up and down so that sometimes they could look out over the fjord and were almost level with it and at other times it was hidden behind high rocks.

'Keep looking on your left,' ordered the Tigress when they had reached a certain point on the journey. 'The rock is somewhere here.' Eagerly they kept their eyes peeled.

'*There!*' ejaculated Sanders suddenly. They had all seen it. Silhouetted against the clear sky was a rock shaped with the evil curved beak and rounded head of a falcon. The Tigress pulled in by the roadside and for a while there was silence as they stared upwards at the spectacle. The surface of the rock was chipped and scarred, giving a feathery effect, and there was a cave forming an eye.

'I don't suppose any of you are desperate to stay here and guard the children – you all want to be there when we find the jewels, I presume,' said the

Tigress with a trace of a smile. 'Besides, I don't trust any of you to look after them for a minute. They will come with us.' Everyone climbed out of the van and the doors clanged shut. 'If you are sensible you will behave yourselves,' the Tigress warned the cousins, who were looking round hopefully.

They all began scrambling up over the rocks. Rubble crumbled and rolled away under their feet, and John and Michelle each stumbled twice, for it was very steep. At last they reached the neck of the falcon's head.

'Where can you hide jewels here?' asked Dudgeon between gasps. The Tigress's sharp eyes scanned the rock.

'The eye,' she said. 'It's a cave. In there.'

With even more difficulty they scrambled to the large recess. It was full of cracks and rubble. A pyramid of light let in by the small entrance rested on the cave floor, which was matted with pulverised rock and broken bits of stone. The men began to brush away rubble excitedly. The cousins watched with a mixture of fascination and distaste. As the men scrabbled about their hair clung to their faces with sweat. The Tigress's expression was cool, but John noticed that she was nervously twisting round a ring on her middle finger.

'*Here*!' gasped Rumsey at last. Behind a huge pile of rubble near the bottom of the cave wall was a tiny horizontal hole. A piece of dirty cloth was visible if one laid one's head on the ground next to it. The others hurried over to Rumsey, who was kneeling in flakes of rock surrounded by piles of dust and rubble. He squeezed his hand into the hole while Hackett breathed impatiently down his neck, a wicked gleam in his eye. It took several attempts before Rumsey's fingertips caught hold of a pinch of the cloth and he tugged it out. The villains' eyes sparkled with greed and excitement as a bulky parcel in a dusty cloth bag was pulled out. To Rumsey's annoyance, Hackett snatched it and his fingers fumbled with the neck. Then he tipped some of the contents into his grubby palm. Jewels sparkled in his hand and several spilled to the floor.

'Diamonds!' gasped Dudgeon. 'And – and – yellow things . . .' The jewels had no settings. They were of all sizes, shapes and colours. In the dim light of the cave they glinted and glistened. But the Tigress snatched a palmful of the stones suspiciously. She examined them, scratched them together and placed one coloured one between two flat rocks. When she lifted the upper rock they saw that the stone had been almost pulverised. A cold glazed look crossed the Tigress's face. For a moment there was a tense silence.

'NO! Not paste!' wailed Sanders.

'*Yes*,' snarled the Tigress savagely and flung the fake jewels she held at the cave wall with such force and fury that some of them cracked. Deceitfully gleaming, the paste jewels clattered to the floor and into the dirt and dust. '*The pig*! THE DOUBLE-CROSSING PIG!' roared the Tigress, her fingers stiff as if she wanted to claw her enemy's eyes out with her long nails. 'I'll KILL him! And now, *he* makes off with the real jewels. After *all this trouble*! The – the – the – I'll KILL him!' Now her voice was hoarse with rage and utter loathing.

Coker, whimpering, began to hunt behind more rubble, hoping they had found the wrong jewels. Hackett exploded. And he decided to take it out on John and Michelle.

'Those kids!' he bawled. 'They've brought us nothing but bad luck! I'll kill THEM!'

'No. We need that ransom more than ever now,' Sanders said.

'SHUUURRUUP!' screeched Hackett madly. While his gaze was on Sanders and the others were fuming or gaping in dismay, the cousins suddenly darted out of the cave and began to scramble over the falcon's beak. They half slid, half climbed down the other side with the furious gang after them. Michelle went over on her ankle but hobbled on and John fell and scraped his face on a rock, but on they stumbled. Then to their indescribable horror they found that they were on a wide ledge of rock which jutted out over the fjord. The only way of escape was over the edge and down – down – down – over the cliff . . . perhaps plunging to death . . . The gang were approaching – walking now. They knew the cousins were trapped. And Hackett had his gun out.

'Don't be a fool, Hackett,' snarled the Tigress, catching his arm. 'The ransom's all we've got left.' But, for once, Hackett ignored her and approached the cousins menacingly. The mad look in his eyes terrified them. They backed away towards the cliff edge. Michelle glanced over her shoulder and shuddered as she saw the perilous drop to the water – such a drop that it could kill them. Their feet were centimetres from the very cliff edge. And then, not having looked behind him, John took another small step backwards. His foot was on the very edge of the cliff; but suddenly the unsafe rock crumbled and his foot was in mid-air. With a cry he overbalanced backwards! Absentmindedly and in terror he grabbed at Michelle's arm. But it was too late. He succeeded only in pulling his cousin with him! With gasps of panic they both tumbled backwards and down . . . !

chapter nine

The Missing Letter

The drop was the most terrifying thing that had happened to either of them in their lives. Down they zoomed in an icy gush of air which streamed through their hair and rushed harshly up over their faces and surged into their aching throats – the cliff flashed by and all was blurred, their muscles were tense with terror, they had lost all sense of balance ... Down ... down ... the nightmare fall hurled them into the water with a tremendous impact after they had gasped in what they dreaded was their last breath of air. All they could see were bubbles and frothing salt water which tried to choke them. Into the depths of the cold, clutching fjord they sank, despite their struggling. Down ... down ... at last they began to float up through the dark depths but already feeling dizzy and on the verge of drowning. They knew it was a long, long way to the surface but – if only they could make it ... John kicked with his legs to speed up the rising but his attempts were weak; for his whole chest and throat were stretched and agonising. His lungs felt as if they would burst the next second and he was dizzy and faint, with an incessant buzzing in his vibrating head. Surely the surface was near now.

But no; and John couldn't breathe! He began to panic, kicking wildly and waving his arms. Terror tightened his muscles even more. He thought he was dead and then realised he wasn't. He was feeling sick and half stunned. Desperate for air he opened his mouth, praying that the water would turn to oxygen. But the cold sea cruelly gushed into his throat. The pain in his head was unbearable. He gave up. At that moment his head broke the surface of the water and he gasped in air. Choking and coughing, not fully conscious, he desperately made an attempt to tread water. His head buzzed, throbbed and ached and all his muscles felt torn apart. Surely he was not alive! It must be another place – another world. When he opened his eyes the water under his lashes stung them and made everything bleary. He was still choking, and tormented with anxiety for Michelle. He had avoided death only by a whisker; if she had been under ten seconds longer . . . If Michelle was dead he didn't want to be alive. He scanned the sun-glazed water with strained hope, his eyes still bleary. Then a hand clutched his wet shirt at the back under the water, and a hoarse, cracked voice, almost inaudible, whispered, 'John.' Weak with relief he turned in the water. Only her head was visible above the surface. Her white face was mottled with blue, her lashes beaded with water drops, her pale lips quivering with shock. She hung on to him with trembling hands, too weak to stay afloat by herself.

'I thought you were dead,' he whispered, shivering with cold.

'No, I'm still alive, thank God.' Suddenly remembering, John glanced up to the clifftop. One of the men, small and dark in the distance, was still there, but the other four and the Tigress were gone!

'They'll be coming after us,' John said, tense with the shock of reality. Beyond the sheer cliff face, the land dipped down to form a rocky bay. 'We must get ashore and find help.'

'John, have mercy,' Michelle begged. 'I can't swim, at least not now.' She was still gasping for breath between words.

'I'm sorry, but we must. Please try,' he urged.

'No, please. I can't,' she whimpered, bowing her head and still clutching his arms for support.

'But if we don't they'll be on the shore waiting for us – and Hackett with his gun.'

'It's all horrid, *horrid*,' she mumbled, shivering. 'I don't want to believe it. It's not true, John, tell me it's not.'

'You've got to face up to reality – especially now,' John told her firmly and a little impatiently. 'You'll get us both killed if you don't come. Please don't be silly. Now, I'll help you. You're suffering from shock.'

'I'm sorry,' she said, bravely breaking into breast-stroke. 'I'm a stupid baby.'

'Save your breath for swimming,' gasped John. After inhaling, Michelle turned her stroke to a rather haphazard front crawl and they struck out for the rocky shore. John's strength was coming back to him, although Michelle's front crawl was nothing to write home about. She was hardly kicking at all and her arms just slowly beat the water. She was sure it was only a matter of time before she breathed her last. But when the shore was only a few metres away she managed to force herself on, and they sank on to the cool rocks, panting hard.

'This – this is a-about the third time we've been soaked through,' Michelle observed, and sneezed violently. John hoisted her to her feet.

'Come on. We've got to get help before they find us.'

'B-but – '

'Look, over there is a village.'

'Where?'

John pointed.

'But it's so small we can hardly see it – it's *miles* away.'

'Well, there must be some houses nearer. We'll head that way anyhow. What else can we do? If we bump into Hackett or see that blue van we're as good as done for.'

'OK,' Michelle agreed with an effort. 'But I can't run or walk fast.'

'Oh, yes! I forgot – you did something to your ankle. Is it OK?'

'It's nothing.'

'We might bump into some tourists,' John said hopefully as they picked their way over loose stones and vegetation towards a thin dusty track between the rocks. But the only mammal life they saw was a stray sheep with a bell jingling round its neck.

'We've got enough information to put all those

crooks in jail for years,' Michelle said as they tramped on.

'Yes,' John agreed, shivering in his drenched attire. 'But who do you think hid those fake jewels, and why?'

'It must have been the same person who put the code on the lockets for Cox, Evans, Yates and Grier,' Michelle deduced. 'And I think that he was probably the Tigress's brother, Webb. Remember how the gang said that the Tigress got to know about the lockets from Webb, and that she'd stolen his code papers? If it was Webb's code on the lockets, he probably put it there and sent them.'

'Maybe,' agreed John.

'But why did he want to lead Cox, Evans, Yates and Grier to paste jewels?'

'Haven't a clue,' admitted John. 'But I think – gosh – look!' A good distance away, winding round the hairpin bends, was a dark blue van. The cousins ducked down behind a large rock. The van was as small as a toy car in the distance, but John and Michelle were not going to risk being seen. Once again they were tense with nerves as they clutched the rock and peeped round the side. Then to their immense relief the van disappeared behind some rocks. But still there was danger. It might reappear before long.

'Let's go!' whispered John. 'We can't stay here all the time. I think the farther away we are from Falcon's Head Rock the better.' They hurried on, glancing round apprehensively. Tired and weary, they kept going until neither of them could continue. They sank down behind another rock, resting their buzzing heads on their arms while their hearts furiously pumped out insufficient energy.

'Not much farther,' John panted.

'What?' queried his cousin incredulously, her eyes wandering to the distant village, which was cradled between the mountains above the sleek, sinuous water of the blue fjord.

'Up there is a little hut. Can you see it?' Michelle's eyes brightened. Sure enough, higher up, nestling between some trees was a dark brown wooden house with a turf roof and a patch of grass round it.

'Come on,' urged John. They stumbled on, praying that the blue van would not appear. Puffing and panting, they reached the wooden house with its sun-drenched turf roof and one stone step at the door. John knocked loudly, glancing round apprehensively for the blue van. The door swung open and a small man with long wispy grey hair and sharp curious eyes peered at them. He was rolling up the sleeves of his pale grey shirt, revealing plump brown arms.

'Excuse me,' John said, 'but could we come in? You see . . . er . . .'

The man's brown face creased as he frowned suspiciously. 'British tourists?' he asked. He spoke quickly and sharply. His large dignified Roman nose did not seem to go with the rest of his face, the shrivelled cheeks and pointed chin.

'Not tourists. We were brought here by criminals.'

'Criminals?' the man asked incredulously and

gave a short laugh at what he believed to be an outrageous tale. He began rolling up his other sleeve. His eyes were never still. 'It seems to me that you young British tourists are up to some trickery. What is it that you have really come for?'

'It's a long story,' John said anxiously. 'If we could come in . . .' The man looked completely uninterested and was absorbed in his sleeves. 'You see,' John began, 'we were kidnapped in Britain. We came here – '

'Look!' sighed the man, throwing up his hands impatiently. 'I have no time for – '

'We were brought here,' continued John stormily, refusing to be stopped again, 'because the criminals were looking for stolen jewels hidden at Falcon's Head Rock. They discovered paste jewels. We escaped and now they're after us . . .' At the last few sentences the man positively started and looked up alarmed. His indifferent attitude had instantly vanished and his grey eyes moved restlessly to and fro, full of fear.

'What? What is this you say?' he asked shakily. 'Paste jewels? Criminals coming *here*?'

'Well, coming after us,' John explained.

'They are here? Go – *go*! You must leave my home. If they come here . . . *Leave*, I say!'

'But – ' began Michelle. Suddenly the man started again as if he remembered something.

'No, wait,' he said nervously, waving them inside. 'Come in quickly. I have a letter. I do not remember where it is – what I did with it. Help me find it quickly. Then I will take you to find help

– to the village nearby. It is in a blue – er – envelope, the letter. My name is on it – Gustav Johann.
Quick, quick!' He ushered the bewildered cousins
into a room with scrubbed wooden panels, frilled
muslin curtains looped back, carved wooden cup-
boards and chests, and other pieces of wooden furniture. Searching for a letter was not what the
cousins had bargained for, but it seemed they
would receive help when it was found and they
didn't fancy tramping all the way to the village.
Gustav Johann was clearly not as tidy as most
Norwegians. There were books, papers and pencil
stumps scattered over tabletops, and cupboard
doors left open revealing disorderly piles of magazines and old photographs.

'It is probably in here,' Johann told them, frantically burrowing into a pile of papers on a chair
seat. He could not hide his panic. The cousins
reluctantly tackled the books and other articles on
the table. No wonder Johann had lost a letter in
this mess. But the cousins were very puzzled and
suspicious. What was this letter? Why was it so
important? And why had Gustav Johann's manner
changed so suddenly when they had mentioned fake
jewels at Falcon's Head Rock as if he knew about
it? He didn't seem to have noticed that the cousins
were wet through. He just wanted this letter! And
why was he so frightened? John started on a cupboard. He was becoming impatient. He tossed
papers over his shoulder on to the floor as Johann
was doing. The boy was just about to do the same
with a blue envelope when he realised it was what

they were looking for. But suspicion was nagging at John. What *was* this letter? He was not in the habit of reading people's private correspondence, but this was an exception, and John was determined to find out the reason for Johann's strange behaviour. He sighed, 'This is hopeless. I'm going to look in another room.' Johann did not say anything. His brow was furrowed with anxiety. John went into the hall and took out the letter. His eyes widened as he scanned the paper. The letter read:

Dear Gustav,

   Pleased to hear you have received your payment and safely placed the package at the Falcon's Head Rock. A nice surprise for my four old friends! I am afraid that I shall not be seeing you again this year as I shall be leaving for S. America as soon as I can. Thanks for all your past services. Remember to burn this letter when you have read it, for the sake of us both.

                     Yours sincerely,
                     Jasper Webb.

Webb, thought John! So Webb was going to South America with the real jewels. He had bribed Johann to place the bag of paste jewels at Falcon's Head Rock. And now Johann was afraid the crooks might chase the cousins to his home and see the letter he had forgotten to burn lying around. Suddenly John heard voices outside. He crossed to the hall window and froze. Approaching the house was the Tigress's gang!

146

chapter ten

Chase On The Mountains

'Michelle! They're coming! The Tigress and Hack-ett!' John cried hoarsely. In a flash Michelle and Gustav Johann were in the hall. Johann was pale and worried.

'Get out of my house!' ordered the man. 'You bring me danger! Go, I say!'

'I wish we could,' John told him shakily. But they could not leave without being seen by their former captors.

'We'll have to hide!' Michelle gasped, turning pale. John glanced at the large table next to the front door. He tore into the dining-room, whisked a tablecloth off the table and dashed back into the hall.

'Wait! You have my letter. Give it to me!' Johann cried. John took no notice but spread the cloth over the hall table.

'Get under!' he told Michelle. He crawled after her and they crouched there hidden by the table-cloth which reached to the floor, praying they would not be found.

'Act normally,' John hissed to Johann. The front door shook as Hackett pounded on it. Stiff with worry and nerves, the cousins heard Johann open the door. All six crooks stood before the panicky Norwegian.

'We're looking for our two children,' the cousins heard the Tigress say coolly. 'We have been mountain-climbing and the children ran on ahead. Now we have lost them and are very anxious in case they have had an accident. This is the only house around, so we hoped you might have seen them. There is a boy, tall and fair, wearing jeans and a pale shirt. The girl has long brownish hair. She was wearing a skirt and red blouse. Have you seen them by any chance?' The cousins held their breath. Would Johann give them away?

'I am sorry,' he apologised. 'I have seen no one but you today. I stay indoors because I do not like the heat. I have a home near Bergen but I come here in the summer. I am sorry. I hope your children will be all right.' He sounded a trifle shaky.

'Are you *sure* you haven't seen them?' prodded the Tigress coldly.

'Yes, yes, quite sure. Two children in their teens – a boy and a girl you say? No, I haven't seen them.'

John winced as the Tigress demanded, 'Then how did you know they were in their teens? I didn't tell you.'

'Oh, well – I – er – just thought they might be . . .'

'I think we'd better come in,' drawled Hackett menacingly.

'N-no,' faltered Johann. 'You can't just barge into my home.'

'Can't we?' sneered Hackett. Footsteps sounded in the hall and the front door slammed shut.

'I know nothing! Who are you?' cried Johann. The voices faded away slightly as the party moved out of the hall. Still clutching Webb's letter, John peeped cautiously from under the tablecloth.

'Come on,' he whispered. They crept out and John quietly opened the front door, both of them terrified that someone would re-enter the hall. The door clicked when they shut it and they breathed thankfully. But they might not be safe yet. They hurried through the trees and up a scarred rocky slope. Suddenly both of them jumped as a voice shouted quite a distance behind them. They both swung round abruptly, stiff with a terrible dread. Their faces tightened with fear as they saw Hackett pointing at them fiercely, with the Tigress and the other men at his side.

'*Run!*' gasped John chokily. They scrambled over the rocks, stumbling and slipping and panicking. Both had lumps in their throats. When they glanced feverishly over their shoulders they saw Sanders, Hackett and Rumsey hurrying after them with the Tigress gingerly picking her way along behind in her high-heeled boots. Dudgeon and Coker were not in sight, but the speed and energy with which Hackett, Rumsey and Sanders were chasing the cousins was very alarming. John and Michelle had not forgotten the guns. They must not let themselves get into firing range; they must keep behind cover. They headed for some trees and wound in and out of the thick trunks. Branches and leaves brushed over their heads. Their breath came in choking gasps of terror. They kept glancing back and saw shadows through the trees. Soon they could not see the men in the leafy shade but stumbled on, gasping and panting, wishing they could flop down on to the ground. Suddenly a figure emerged from the trees and clapped an arm round Michelle's neck, holding her in a headlock. Over her shoulder she saw Coker's grim face. Desperate to get away, she writhed and started to scream hysterically. The shrieking rent the air.

As John rushed to help his cousin, Coker shouted, 'Someone come! Hurry!' He could not contend with the struggling girl *and* John. He clapped a hand over Michelle's mouth to stop the screaming and she bit into it very hard. As Coker snatched his offended hand away, she kicked him on the shin and rammed her elbow into his solar plexus. With a yell of pain he let go of her and both cousins dashed off. They heard pounding footsteps behind them and hardly dared to look back. When they did, they saw Sanders in the lead, his face crimson and set with determination. They forced themselves on. Michelle was positive she would die of exhaustion. It was ten times worse than the eight hundred metres, she thought afterwards. They kept falling; both felt faint and dizzy. They came out of the trees, running in sweat, to a wide mountain road. They were tearing across it when Michelle stumbled and was too breathless to get up. This was the end! And what was more, a car was zooming down the road at that very moment! Michelle forced herself on to her hands and knees when she heard the engine. John frantically waved his arms to try to stop the car. The driver saw him and the vehicle skidded to a halt only a metre away from Michelle.

'What the blazes are you – ?' began the driver, opening the window, shocked at the near accident.

Michelle picked herself up.

'Help!' John gasped, as he opened a door and they both tumbled into the back of the car. 'We're being chased by crooks! They've got guns!' He slammed the door shut and locked it, and the cousins found themselves next to the astonished driver's wife and baby. 'Please move before they see us,' begged John. The urgency in the boy's voice assured the driver that he was not bluffing. The man took no chances; he restarted the engine and the car zoomed away. As it rounded a bend, John thought that he caught sight of a shadowy figure emerging on to the road from the trees, and fervently hoped that the tail-end of the car had not been seen disappearing. He and Michelle were now breathing more easily, but John said worriedly, 'They might have seen us – if they have, they'll come after us in their van. Please drive as quickly as possible – to the nearest police station!'

The driver turned off the pop music which had been blaring away on the radio. 'Could you please explain what on earth – ' he began in astonished tones.

'It's a long story,' interrupted John a trifle impatiently. 'Please keep driving as fast as you can to the nearest police station. I'll tell you as we go along.'

The driver obliged, and he and his wife listened in amazement to what they heard. It turned out that they were tourists from Britain who had only recently arrived in Norway and had read about the cousins' disappearance before coming on holiday. They introduced themselves as Mr and Mrs Allan, and explained that they were staying at a hotel in the nearest town. John kept casting anxious glances through the back window for signs of the blue van.

After some speedy driving, they reached a friendly-looking town. Mr Allan dropped his wife and baby at their hotel before stopping the car outside the police station. Although the Sergeant, like most Norwegians, spoke excellent English, it took the combined efforts of Mr Allan and the cousins, as well as Webb's letter, to convince him that their story was bona fide.

'Now that they've lost the jewels – and us – I expect they'll drive straight back to the plane and try to leave the country,' John suggested.

'Most probably,' agreed the Sergeant. 'We will contact all our forces in the area and set up road-blocks to stop the van. From your description of the van journey, we have a good idea whereabouts the plane must have landed.' He asked the cousins for descriptions of the villains and the van, and for any details they could give of the village where they had met Bergslien. 'Now you are not sure if they saw you being picked up by Mr Allan,' went on the Sergeant. 'If they didn't, they could still be hunting for you near Johann's house. In any case, we need to bring in Johann himself for questioning. We should be very grateful if you and Mr Allan could accompany us, to show us where exactly you were picked up, and to help identify the criminals if they are still roaming about in the area.'

John and Michelle were glad to help in bringing the gang to justice, but they were so exhausted that the drive in the police car with the Sergeant and Mr Allan seemed like a hazy dream. Two more police cars followed them, and, as they drove, the Sergeant called in reinforcements from neighbouring villages on his radio.

When Mr Allan pointed out the spot where the cousins had been rescued, the Sergeant and his three passengers remained by their car while a search began. Uniformed figures moved in and out of the trees, combing the woods where the gang had last been seen. It was not long before the cousins caught sight of Johann being accompanied to a car by two policemen. Then they spent a long period in suspense, as more police cars arrived on the scene, fresh men leapt out nimbly, and the search for the Tigress's gang was extended over a wider area.

After what seemed hours, shouting broke out in the distance, and the cousins were almost hopping with excitement as the five handcuffed men were led towards the police cars. Coker was trembling and whimpering, while the other four wore grim scowls. When they caught sight of John and Michelle, bitter hatred glazed their eyes.

With a remark in Norwegian, one policeman handed the Sergeant two revolvers.

'The guns were found on the men,' the Sergeant explained to the cousins. 'It looks as though these are your kidnappers.'

'They are,' confirmed John. 'But what about the Tigress?'

'Where is she?' the Sergeant demanded of Hackett.

'She tried to trick us,' growled the villain furiously. 'She drove off in the van without us. She's going to leave the country.'

'No, she's not!' the Sergeant informed him. 'We've got roadblocks set up. She's probably been stopped by now.'

'Hope she has,' snarled Rumsey. 'She tried to ditch us.'

Glowering, the men were hustled to police cars. Hackett glared accusingly at the cousins, and growled, 'You'll pay for this!'

'Keep quiet,' snapped a policeman. With a mixture of satisfaction and relief, the cousins watched their former captors being driven away. Then they and Mr Allan climbed into the Sergeant's car and the vehicle sped off.

'So what happens to us now?' John wanted to know.

'Well, your parents will have been contacted,' the Sergeant told them, 'and arrangements will be made for your return to Britain as soon as possible. In the meantime, we can probably make reservations for you at a hotel in the town, just for as long as is necessary.'

'I would recommend the hotel where I'm staying,' Mr Allan suggested. 'If they are staying there, I can make sure they have everything they need.'

'Good idea,' agreed the Sergeant. 'I will have a word with the manager, and ask him to arrange for you youngsters to phone your parents from the hotel.'

After the car journey back to the town, the Sergeant and Mr Allan escorted the cousins to a pleasant room in the hotel. John and Michelle each took a refreshing shower and sat in bathrobes while their clothes were taken to be washed and dried. A friendly maid brought up some new garments – jeans and slightly oversize checked shirts. No sooner had they changed than the receptionist phoned their room, and arranged for a call to be put through to their relieved parents. Mr and Mrs Ward were staying with John's father and mother in Leicester, where they had all been desperately awaiting news. They explained that the Norwegian police had contacted them, and that they were all coming to Norway on the next flight. They hoped to arrive by the late afternoon. While John and Michelle were happily discussing the good news, the Sergeant called at their room.

'The Tigress was picked up at a roadblock,' he told them. 'She was in the van and had been driving very fast. She tried to run, and when she was arrested she fell to cursing her brother – and you! You both did a marvellous job helping us to catch the gang – and Gustav Johann too! You see, we found incriminating evidence at his house, which helps us to connect him with several robberies here in Norway. Down at police headquarters he's crying and whimpering and confessing everything he knows.'

'Have you found out why Webb got him to put fake jewels at Falcon's Head Rock?' asked Michelle.

'Yes, we have,' replied the Sergeant. 'It seems that Webb and his four old friends, Evans, Cox, Yates and Grier, had stolen a large quantity of valuable jewellery. But the British police got on to their trail, so they had to split up suddenly and lie low for a while. The jewellery was all left with Webb so that he could melt down the settings – he is an expert jeweller, you see. He promised to arrange for the other four to get their share later, but then he decided to sell all the jewels himself and keep the money. However, he needed time to sell them all, so to keep Evans, Cox, Yates and Grier out of the way, and to stop them becoming suspicious, he planned to send them on a wild-goose chase to Norway; so he engraved the lockets and sent them one each, telling them to meet, work out the code and collect their share of the jewels together; then he paid Johann to plant the fake jewels at the Falcon's Head Rock, hoping that they would be taken in by them, at least for a time. Of course, as only part of the code was on each locket, all four had to get together before they could work out the message. All this was to give Webb more time to dispose of the real jewels, and also to make Cox, Evans, Yates and Grier think that he wasn't double-crossing them, but was being very careful to prevent any of them from finding out the hiding-place on his own and from getting more than his share of the jewels.'

'And the Tigress got to know about the lockets because she's Webb's sister and spies on him,' Michelle put in eagerly.

'Yes, that's right,' replied the Sergeant. 'Her real name is Charis Webb, by the way. She's so furious with her brother that she's told us where the British police can find him in London. Johann doesn't think he'll have left for South America yet. It seems that Charis Webb overheard her brother phoning one of his accomplices with instructions about the lockets just after he'd sent them off, and she never suspected that he was double-crossing them. She found out the addresses of Cox, Evans, Yates and Grier, and got hold of a copy of the code system which Webb used with them, and gave it to Hackett. Webb must have taken good care not to let her find out that the hiding-place was Falcon's Head Rock, so she had to get hold of the lockets. And he must have kept the real jewels well hidden from her all the time he had them.'

There was a pause while the cousins turned all this over in their minds.

'It wouldn't surprise me,' went on the Sergeant, 'if Webb didn't deliberately let her overhear about the lockets, to keep her out of his way, as well as his four accomplices. From what she and Johann have told us, it seems that the brother and sister were always trying to get the better of each other.'

'Webb sounds a very crafty specimen,' John observed. 'By the way, what will happen to Cox, Grier and Yates? I don't suppose you've heard anything about them from Britain?'

'We have informed the British police, who may be able to locate Grier's farm,' replied the Sergeant. 'They might need some help or information from you when you get home – I don't know.'

'Have you heard that our parents are on their way here?' John asked. 'They should arrive this afternoon.'

'That's splendid! Well, you must be ready for some lunch in the restaurant – it's all been arranged.' He opened the door to go. 'I'll see you soon, I expect.'

On the way down to the restaurant John looked thoughtful.

'There's one thing I'm still wondering about,' he said. 'How do you suppose Evans knew he was being chased by Hackett's Mercedes?'

Michelle shrugged. 'I expect he must have bumped into the five of them earlier, and then somehow got away before he had his accident.'

'Yes, that must be it,' John agreed.

When they entered the restaurant, where there was a continuous buzz of chatter, a jolly waiter approached them with an ingratiating grin.

'John and Michelle?' he enquired.

'Yes, that's right,' grinned John. They were given seats at a long table next to the Allans and some friendly American tourists. They had a pleasant chat with the Allans and Americans while they ate their first course, which was a huge plate of herring.

When the cousins had finished they were surprised to see the Americans starting on another main course.

'Didn't you know?' grinned Mrs Allan. 'In Norway they *expect* you to eat three or four main courses, then go on to about three puddings. The Norwegians are great eaters.'

Twenty minutes later John forced down the last piece of meat on his plate and the next moment was staring in horror at another plate piled with a *smörbröd*, made of single slices of bread upon which rose pyramids of meat, fish, cheese, egg, tomato, lettuce . . .

'The main meal of the day is in the evening,' remarked one of the Americans. 'They eat more then!'

John and Michelle staggered out of the restaurant, their stomachs seeming seven times as big as they had been when they entered.

'I feel absolutely bloated,' gasped John, and then added with a satisfied smile, 'but it was *delicious*.'

They went up to their room and spent the afternoon relaxing. Then the Sergeant appeared at the door.

'Hello! Did you have a good lunch? Your parents should be here any minute now.'

'Great! Let's go and wait for them at the main entrance,' suggested Michelle with enthusiasm. They did, and were soon standing in the warm sunlight, looking eagerly along the road.

'Oh!' John cried, clapping his hand to his head as he suddenly remembered. 'That's something I must ask Dad!'

'What?'

'Who won the Test Match, of course!'